LA LOCA DE GANDOCA /
THE MADWOMAN OF GANDOCA

LA LOCA DE GANDOCA / *THE MADWOMAN OF GANDOCA*

Anacristina Rossi

Translated by
Terry J. Martin

The Edwin Mellen Press
Lewiston•Queenston•Lampeter

Library of Congress Cataloging-in-Publication Data

Rossi, Anacristina
  [Loca de Gandoca. English]
  La loca de Gandoca = The madwoman of Gandoca / Anacristina Rossi ; translated by
Terry J. Martin
      p. cm.
  Includes bibliographical references and index.
  ISBN-13: 978-0-7734-5637-2
  ISBN-10: 0-7734-5637-6
  I. Martin, Terry J. II. Title. III. Title: Madwoman of Gandoca.

PQ7489.2.R59L6313 2006
863'.64--dc22

                                                                    2006046976
hors série.

A CIP catalog record for this book is available from the British Library.

The Edwin Mellen Press	The Edwin Mellen Press
Box 450	Box 67
Lewiston, New York	Queenston, Ontario
USA 14092-0450	CANADA L0S 1L0

The Edwin Mellen Press, Ltd.
Lampeter, Ceredigion, Wales
UNITED KINGDOM SA48 8LT

Printed in the United States of America

In memory of my mother Myrna S. Martin, who inspired in me a love of nature.

Table of Contents

Preface

Holding this fine translation of *La loca de Gandoca* in hand, I am reminded of another madwoman, one who also would not remain in the attic but insisted on entering the public sphere and disrupting the plans of others. But more than the Bertha imagined by Charlotte Brontë, I think of her earlier incarnation at the hands of Jean Rhys, who recognized that being uprooted from one's soil can drive someone mad. As in Daniela's case, that younger Bertha's life is also defined by the lush ecology of tropical latitudes. But whereas that Bertha was uprooted from the soil that gave life to her native vegetation, Daniela faces the uprooting of that very vegetation and the destruction of that living soil at the hands of developers and corrupt politicians. She, too, lights a fire, but rather than a self-destructive one that only damages the manor house, hers is a self-regenerative and socially constructive fire that burns away the veil that hides the enemies of the people and the enemies of the environment, both the land and the waters around it, from view.

In addition to thinking about *The Madwoman of Gandoca*'s character, I am also led to think about her author, herself a fire starter, an activist author, whose words prove so powerful that vested interests threatened her with death in an effort to silence her protests. But they were too late, as her novel had already initiated a long, loud struggle that continues in Anacristina Rossi's Costa Rica today. She herself reminds me of other authors. First, the Japanese writer, Ishimure Michiko, who worked tirelessly for many years to expose the horrors of Minimata disease and the organic mercury industrial pollution that caused it. Her book, *Paradise in the Sea of Sorrow*, also available to English-language readers in an excellent translation, became a required high school text in her home country and remains a beautiful tribute to the victims of that disease as well as a searing exposé of the corporation and government bureaucrats who denied and then attempted to evade their responsibility for so much human suffering and environmental degradation. Second, the American writer, Carl Hiaasen, whose uproarious novels about Florida politics and economic development share the same postmodern sensibility and wickedly effective humor found in The Madwoman. It is a tribute to Terry Martin's skills as a translator that he is able to capture and carry over the pointed and politically effective humor of Rossi's Spanish into American English. Hiaasen and Rossi are, in fact, kindred spirits in many ways because they address the same kinds of issues about runaway development, government corruption, and environmental scams in their fiction. I think of such novels by Hiaasen in this regard as *Skinny Dip*, *Stormy Weather*, and *Sick Puppy*. These three authors, Rossi, Ishimure, and Hiaasen, form part of an international body of contemporary writers using the power of popular fiction to expose environmental injustices around the world.

This translation is much needed because, in truth, far too little attention is given to the role of fiction in helping to shape public opinion about environmental issues and matters of environmental justice. Terry Martin's translation will enable Rossi's *The Madwoman of Gandoca* to take its place on the shelves of environmental activists and concerned citizens throughout the English-reading world, alongside such works as *Silent Spring*, *Refuge*, *Appalachian Autumn*, *My Year of Meats*, *Track of the Cat*, *So Far From God*, *Zodiac*, and other novels and nonfiction books that inspire individuals and remind them both of the need for environmental activism and the tremendous stakes in each and every battle for a particular ecosystem, shoreline, animal refuge, or individual backyard.

This translation is also needed because it adds another volume to the growing international body of literature that accurately and appropriately unites ecology and feminism–ecofeminism–in their mutual recognitions of the destructive ideological forces and oppressive and exploitative social systems that undergird each of these battles. Martin's translation successfully and pleasurably captures the gendered nuances of Rossi's style. And his translation takes on further importance because we have far too few Latin American literary works being translated outside of a relatively narrowly defined stylistic canon and set of anticipated themes, even though an ever-expanding body of Latin American and Caribbean environmental literature is available and needs to be brought to the attention of English-only readers.

In short, Terry Martin has performed a significant service to readers and to environmental justice by translating Anacristina Rossi's *La loca de Gandoca*. He provides English-language readers with a translation that captures the humor, poignancy, and political pathos of a masterwork of ecofeminist fiction. It is precisely the kind of text I will be using when I teach for the first time next year the undergraduate course I have designed for my university's environmental studies minor, "The International Literature of Environmental Justice."

Patrick Murphy

Patrick D. Murphy is Professor of English at the University of Central Florida. Founding editor of ISLE: Interdisciplinary Studies in Literature and Environment, he is the author, among other works, of *Farther Afield in the Study of Nature-Oriented Literature* and *Literature, Nature, Other: Ecofeminist Critiques*. He has also edited and co-edited such books as *The Literature of Nature: An International Sourcebook* and *Ecofeminist Literary Criticism*. He is currently working on a study of nature in contemporary American novels and editing a volume devoted to transnational ecocritical theory.

Acknowledgments

Literary endeavors invariably depend on a web of relationships. I wish to extend warm thanks to Anacristina Rossi for her help in translating certain challenging technical terms and idiomatic expressions, as well as for her invaluable critical advice on the style of the translation. I would also like to thank Baldwin-Wallace College for a Faculty Development Summer Grant I received in 2000, which helped made this work possible. In addition, I thank my ex-wife Toty Martin for her gracious support and understanding during the writing of the manuscript, as well as for her suggestions on the translation of key terms. Special thanks to Sofía Kearns for permission to use the cover photograph, which she took of the beach at the Gandoca-Manzanillo Wildlife Refuge. Finally, I would like to thank the many readers of my manuscript who provided helpful comments, including Sofía Kearns, Patrick Murphy, Janet Joseph, Margarita Vargas, María Marín my sister Tris M. Dunn, my father Don Martin, and my late mother Myrna S. Martin.

Introduction

The publication of *La loca de Gandoca* in 1992 unleashed an unprecedented national dialogue in Costa Rica on the relationship between conservation and economic development. A literary, ecological, political and legal text, it continues to stir thought and emotion today, when cases similar to the one it portrays are happening in the country and around the globe. With twelve editions sold out to date, it is one of the most successful publications in Costa Rica in recent times.

La loca de Gandoca brought national attention to the Gandoca-Manzanillo Wildlife Refuge (GMWR, referred to as "Gandoca" in the novel), a remote place on the southern tip of Limón, the Caribbean province of Costa Rica. It narrates the events leading to a real-life environmental and legal case, through which residents of that area tried to save the refuge from imminent commercialization and eventual destruction. The novel was written hastily—in just four months—after every legal channel available to defend and save the refuge had been tried. The purpose of the novel was to blow the whistle on political corruption that threatened the destruction of the refuge.

Award-winning author Anacristina Rossi became well known in 1986 when her novel *María la noche* won the Aquileo Echeverría National Prize. The success of this first novel went beyond national borders and was soon translated into French. In 1993, a year after the publication of *La loca de Gandoca*, she published *Situaciones conyugales*, a collection of short stories, some of which furthered her inquiry into the environmental destruction and loss of cultural identity in Costa Rica. One story of this collection, "Pasión vial," translated as "Highway Passion," was later published in the United States. *Limón Blues*, her latest novel, published in 2002, celebrates Afro-Caribbean cultural and historical heritage in Costa Rica and has won several prestigious awards, among them the 2002 *Ancora* and National Prizes, and the 2004 Casa de las Américas' José María Arguedas prize.

La loca de Gandoca is a fine example of "*testimonio*," or "testimonial literature," which has a long tradition in Latin America, closely related to a unique cultural aspect and a deeply held belief: that literature has the power to change society. *Testimonios*, which often include autobiographical information and a combination of fact and fiction, usually denounce a real-life situation, which the author seeks to change. The tradition of testimonial literature acquired unprecedented importance in the seventies and eighties, when many *testimonios* by women were published. The most widely read was perhaps *I, Rigoberta Menchú: an Indian woman in Guatemala*, edited and introduced by Elisabeth Burgos-Debray.

La loca de Gandoca takes the form of an autobiographical account, narrated in the first person of the protagonist-narrator. The format of a conversation is apparent through the targeting of the narration to the protagonist's dead husband, to whom the story of the events unfolding in Gandoca is told. Its central theme, which is the plea for the conservation of nature, sets *La loca de Gandoca* apart from previous *testimonios*, as well as, indeed, from traditional Latin American literature. The woman protagonist identifies deeply with nature in its many facets of resiliency, strength, and vulnerability. Her voice questions Costa Rican patriarchy and its assumption that nature, women, and the minority populations of Limón are at best secondary entities subordinate to the interests of the white male ruling class of the Central Valley.

The novel also belies the commercial image of Costa Rica as "the perfect eco-tourism destination" and allows the reader to see a more complete, albeit complicated, picture of the country. Costa Rica is, indeed, one of the world's main destinations for ecological tourism, and among Latin American countries, a model for its National Park system and its environmental laws and regulations.

This is a truly amazing achievement for a so-called third-world country, whose main source of revenue until the early nineties was the banana industry. Environmental awareness has been central to Costa Rica for generations for several reasons. Its geographical configuration produces an amazing number of habitats, appropriate for many different kinds of plant and animal species. According to the 1995 World Resources Institute, Costa Rica has the highest biodiversity in the world, with 615 species per every 10,000 square kilometers. (By comparison, the number of species in the entire United States is 104 per every 10,000 sq. km.) This natural wealth, mostly concentrated in the rainforests, the richest habitats in the world, has attracted scientists worldwide since the early twentieth century, many of whom set up agricultural and ecological research programs in the country. These programs have undoubtedly contributed to the education of Costa Ricans and foreigners, scientists and lay persons alike, on the importance of ecosystems and biodiversity. Furthermore, historical developments in Costa Rica since colonial times also contributed to the fact that many pristine habitats remain. Costa Rica was never a political, economic, or cultural center, and, therefore, industrial development arrived later than in other Latin American countries, which meant that large-scale destruction of its natural resources occurred at a slower pace.

Although Costa Rica's natural beauty and conservation achievements deserve to be recognized and applauded, Rossi's novel reveals that they are endangered by the corruption of government officials, whose policies (both legal and otherwise) have contributed to massive ongoing deforestation. The Gandoca-Manzanillo Wildlife Refuge was not threatened until relatively recently, when it was "discovered" by investors determined to exploit it. Though small in size, the refuge is a place of beauty, and of ecological, and cultural importance. Located at the southern extreme of the Caribbean coast of Costa Rica, and comprising 9,449 hectares, 4,436 of which are marine, it is part of the Talamanca/Caribbean Biological Corridor, the only strip of forest connecting the Talamanca coast with the high mountains of the La Amistad Biosphere Reserve. It was created in 1985 to protect the magnificent coral reefs, which extend up to 200 meters off shore for a total of 5 square kilometers. These coral reefs are of great ecological value for their biodiversity. The refuge also protects patches of primary and secondary rainforest, and a 400-hectare swamp with mostly holillo and sajo palms (*Raphia taedigera* and *Campnosperma panamensis*). The Gandoca estuary is made up almost exclusively of red mangrove (*Rhizophora mangle*), which is a tarpon spawning ground and a manatee habitat.

Culturally, the lands of the refuge and their surrounding area display a rich diversity that the rest of the country lacks. Indigenous people inhabited the place long before the Spanish conquistadors arrived, and today live in the reservations set aside for them by the government. The Bribris, one of the most important groups, live close to the GMWR in the Cocles or Kékõldi Reserve. Afro-Caribbeans from Panama (Colombia) and Nicaragua hunted sea turtles on the Costa Rican coast from the early years of the 19th century, eventually establishing permanent settlements at Cahuita, Puerto Viejo (Old Harbour), Punta Uva (Grape Point), Manzanillo, and Punta Mona (Monkey Point). Later in the century, many Jamaicans came to work for the railroad and the banana plantations. Today, Afro-Caribbean people constitute 43% of the population of Limón. They have contributed to the cultural distinctiveness of the area with their language and traditions. Their traditional language is *Mecaitelia*, the local English dialect, which they maintain alongside Standard English and Spanish.

The promotion of ecotourism in Costa Rica started in the eighties and boomed in the nineties. Its many positive aspects may be exemplified by the Baulas de Guanacaste National Park on the Pacific coast, which protects the nesting places of the leather back turtle. Local people, who formerly were egg poachers, have been trained to teach tourists the importance of preserving this habitat. Others now patrol the beaches in order to protect the nests. Obviously, turtles, locals, and tourists benefited enormously from this approach. The basic idea behind ecotourism is brilliant: it invests the revenue obtained from ecotourists in the preservation of the natural places they come to see, thus yielding educational, economic and ecological gains. Ecotourism educates tourists and locals alike on the value and the processes of nature. It brings an economic booster to certain areas, and becomes an incentive to local populations to keep habitats and their biodiversity healthy instead of slashing and burning them, or hunting and selling threatened species for survival. But, as with everything, ecotourism is not perfect, and it has also brought a host of other problems to Costa Rica. *La loca de Gandoca* addresses precisely the potential abuses this industry can foster. The most obvious one is the avalanche of tourists who visit every year to see nature, which, ironically, pushes the building of more infrastructure, often leading to the destruction of more natural areas. In 1989, 376,000 tourists visited Costa Rica. A decade later the number had almost tripled to a staggering 940,000. This boom in the tourist industry, although beneficial to the country's economy, raises questions about the capability of Costa Rica to regulate the impact of humans on nature. Recent studies show that Costa Rica has one of the highest rates of deforestation in the world, with 3.9% of its forested areas being cut each year (about 65,000 hectares, or 160,000 acres). Massive tourism contributes to more deforestation. Another problem with ecotourism, less obvious to visitors, but nevertheless accurately exposed throughout the novel is that, even though Costa Rica boasts so many laws for the protection of its environment, it does not have the resources to enforce them efficiently. This situation makes possible the abuse of nature for profit, even under the guise of ecological purposes.

La loca de Gandoca presents a deep cultural analysis of Costa Rica, discernible on at least three levels: the country's balancing of economic development and conservation, its national identity, and its moral stance towards nature. At the most apparent level, it raises significant questions about the Western paradigm of development under which everything is measured for its ability to yield a profit. Particularly, the novel presents a critique of Neoliberal economic policies adopted by the Costa Rican government during the eighties, which encouraged fast-paced development in diverse areas, particularly pristine beaches, mostly by foreign investors lured to the country by tax exemptions and other generous laws. With exquisite humor and irony, the novel mocks politicians, government officials and investors in their drive for economic gain and their total disregard for nature. A deeper level of inquiry in the novel relates to Costa Ricans' national identity, which, in the narrator's view, is being rapidly lost due to economic and cultural influences from the United States. The novel gives a clear message to Costa Ricans that the loss of land (which is passing quickly into the hands of foreign landowners) and of biodiversity (due to indiscriminate exploitation of the natural resources) will inflict a deep wound in their national identity and ultimately in their soul. At its deepest level of inquiry, the novel poses moral questions not only to Costa Ricans but to all readers, about our stewardship of nature: do diverse and unique species of animals and plants have a right to exist? Where do they go when their habitat is wiped out? Are we humans entitled to exploit nature to the point of extinction? What is, and what should be our ideal relationship with nature? What exactly is wildlife? What is the ideal balance between economic growth and nature conservation? What can and should individuals do against powerful corporations and government officials bent on destroying natural habitats?

The actual case exposed in *La loca de Gandoca* started in 1990, when some residents of the GMWR (wildlife refuges in Costa Rica allow private landowners) began to notice increased clear-cutting and development within the forests of the refuge. Alarmed, they consulted the Ministry of Natural Resources, Energy and Mines (then called MIRENEM, now MINAE) and other governmental entities, such as the Forestry office, in order to find out what was going on. What started as a simple inquiry to government officials about the fate of the refuge, became a year and a half ordeal for Anacristina Rossi and some of her neighbors, which culminated in their exposure of corruption at high governmental levels and in her receiving death threats by corporations and developers. The novel shows how an illegal construction permit was given to the "Eurocaribeña" hotel company (which appears as "Eco-dollars" in the novel) to build a hotel within the lands of the wildlife refuge. On the 17 of June, 1990, then president of Costa Rica Rafael Angel Calderón, known as "the president of the New Ecological order," and the minister of Natural Resources, Energy and Mining, Hernán Bravo Trejos, approved the permit, which was illegal for several reasons. According to Costa Rican law, large-scale projects are not allowed within wildlife refuges, and any such proposals must be preceded by an environmental impact study. Eurocaribeña didn't meet these legal requirements. Furthermore, Rossi got a hold of official documents which showed that Eurocaribeña's proposal to construct a "hotel" merely masked a plan to subdivide a large area of the refuge in order to sell it later to interested entrepreneurs. *La loca de Gandoca* exposed this scheme conceived by certain foreign investors and Costa Rican officials, which, undoubtedly, would have opened the way to rapid deterioration of the fragile ecosystems of the refuge.

The GMWR case would not have achieved the high level of publicity it did had not it been for *La loca de Gandoca*. Its timely publication, at the moment when the Constitutional Tribunal was deciding an appeal that Anacristina Rossi had presented on behalf of the wildlife refuge, instantly fueled an unprecedented national dialogue on the topic of environmental protection vs. development. Almost everyday, between 1992 and 1995, the most important newspapers in the country published an article or editorial on this subject by people as diverse as journalists, lawyers, university professors, students, writers, politicians, biologists, and environmentalists. There is no doubt that this dialogue contributed to a higher awareness among Costa Ricans of the environmental and human situation of the Talamanca coast. For the first time, many Costa Ricans realized the natural wealth comprised by the coral reef, mangroves, swamps, and rainforests of the refuge, as well as the fragility of its ecosystems. And for the first time many of them learned of the problems that black and indigenous communities were facing against big corporate interests and political corruption.

As a *testimonio*, the novel could have not had better results. The impact of the exposé was immediately tangible in official circles as well as at the grass-roots level: first of all, while the legal case was still pending, the Costa Rican government ordered all large-scale construction projects within the refuge to be stopped. The Eurocaribeña project, in particular, was halted permanently. Later, the MIRENEM, and its minister Bravo Trejos, as well as other investors whose projects within the refuge showed irregularities similar to those of the Eurocaribeña proposal, had to answer publicly to the corruption charges stated in the novel. Even though the minister was exonerated later of all charges, this action established a record of the ineptitude and conflicts of interests within the MIRENEM and of the corruption of many high-level government officials. At the grass-roots level, the novel gave a push to a loose ecological movement that had been active at times in the past. Different citizen-driven initiatives sprung up in various areas. For example, residents of the refuge, assisted by the Citizens Commission for Ecological Solutions (Comisión cuidadana de gestión ecológica), created a watch-dog organization in order to check whether new construction projects within the refuge met the ecological standards required by law. And a few years later, the people of Cahuita, a town north of the GMWR, decided to take the lead in the administration of the Cahuita national park, in the jurisdiction of their town.

La loca de Gandoca is a short and powerful text that shows the courage of a woman and other citizens in trying to save the natural landscape they love; their environmental awareness; and the problems they faced for defending a beautiful and rich land. This testimonial novel gives the reader a most complete picture of Costa Rica in the nineties, a transitional time when the country intended to develop economically while attempting to preserve the natural wealth for which it is famous worldwide.

To fully understand and enjoy this testimonial text, a brief explanation of certain legal terms, regulations, and elements unique to the Costa Rican government is necessary, for Rossi takes the reader through the legal and bureaucratic maze she had to navigate in order to save the refuge from development.

The Maritime Zone Law establishes that the 200-meter-wide strip of all coastal land closest to the water is public. The 50 meters closest to the shore (164 feet) are protected from any kind of development. And the remaining 150 meters (492 feet) can be leased from local municipalities. Construction is permitted only if following a Regulating Plan (or Environmental Impact Study), which specifies the type and size of buildings allowed. However, article 73 of the Maritime Law states that this law "doesn't apply in National Parks or equivalent protected areas [such as wildlife refuges], which rather will be regulated by their own legislation." Because article 73 is so unspecific, it allows for diverse and contradicting interpretations. For environmentalists, it implies that stricter regulations will apply in protected lands where the beaches are intended to remain pristine. But according to another interpretation, mostly by private landowners within wildlife refuges, the maritime law does not apply to wildlife refuges, therefore making a Regulating Plan unnecessary. This is the interpretation Rossi had to confront in her effort to save the refuge. Throughout the novel she shows the irrationality of that position according to which coasts within "protected" lands are not protected by any regulations whatsoever.

The Constitutional Tribunal is a special court to which Costa Rican citizens may appeal, if they believe that any of their basic rights under the Costa Rican Constitution or under International Covenants are being violated. The offended party writes a *Recurso de amparo* ("an appeal for help"), to the Constitutional Tribunal, which studies the case and rules on it. In the case of the GMWR, it was Anacristina Rossi who submitted the first *Recurso de amparo,* appealing for environmental laws to be enforced. Her document, written with well-known environmental lawyer Roxana Salazar, presented scientific evidence of the ecological value of the refuge, particularly of its coral reef, and coastal habitats, as a reason for its defense. It urged the government to enforce the existing laws applicable to the refuge, in particular the Environmental Impact Study required for any construction project.

The Arenal Decision was a ruling made by the Constitutional Tribunal before the Gandoca case, which favored private landowners. It determined that they have the right to profit from their land, and that the Costa Rican government will pay compensation if such right is in any way curtailed. Unfortunately, neoliberals, developers, and entrepreneurs seized upon the court's decision to mean that private property could not be regulated, even for purposes such as environmental protection and historical preservation. Because there are private landowners within wildlife refuges, this decision created an unresolved conflict for the GMWR. As clearly exposed throughout the novel, Costa Rican officials invoke the *Arenal Decision* as a shield against any attempts by concerned citizens to enforce environmental laws within the GMWR.

Sofía Kearns

Sofía Kearns is Associate Professor of Spanish at Furman University. She has published articles on the prose of Anacristina Rossi and the poetry of María Mercedes Carranza, Gioconda Belli and Ana María Rodas. Reading *La loca de Gandoca* and hiking in the Gandoca-Manzanillo rainforest was one of the most transforming experiences of her life. The focus of her current research is the relationship between subalternity and environmental awareness in contemporary Latin American literary texts by women.

The Madwoman of Gandoca

For Roxana Salazar and Lenín Corrales

"Listen well, my little daughter, my little dove: the earth is not a place of well being, there is no joy, there is no happiness. It is said that the earth is a place of painful joy, of joy that stings."

The Nahuatl Father's Words to His Daughter
Florentine Codex

You hated boleros, Carlos Manuel. And yet, "suddenly, as in a dream, you came to me."[1]

I barely know you. I'm a single woman with a son, and I arrived a few months ago from Europe. I'm working for now at my brother's shipping agency, and you are the operating manager. It's the Wednesday of Holy Week, and there's no one in the office. Due to certain problems, we have to travel to Puerto Limón together.

The heat is stifling, and we're at the pier checking the papers of the M. V. Clipper Tiger. The captain of the Clipper Tiger is pulling his hair out because they won't let him leave the dock, and he is expected urgently in Guatemala. You swear at the port authority, and I try to contact my brother. After several hours of running between docks and offices, we learn that it was due to a minor oversight of JAPDEVA, the agency in charge of the arrival and departure of ships. We finally get permission to embark.

You approach me with those big yellow-green eyes, shaded by thick, long eyelashes. All afternoon long I've been thinking that one could kill for such eyes. You say in a low voice that the Clipper Tiger is leaving and that our work is done for today. I suppose that your wife is waiting for you somewhere, and I start to say goodbye. But you suddenly add, "Daniela, please, come with me."

"Where?"

"To the most beautiful place in the world."

A note from the author: the characters in this story are imaginary. Any semblance to reality is accidental.

[1] Lyrics from a popular bolero. [Tr.]

You stopped the car, brushed the hair out of my face, and lifted me up. You wound your way between the Raphia palms, and you put me down barefoot on the golden sand beyond them. You knelt down on the beach and said, "Daniela, Daniela, I'm dying of love for you."

I still recall the humidity, the delicious scent of your armpits, and the drenched undulation of the seaweed. You introduced me to the lady of the Atlantic, known as Yemanyá of Benín. "Yemanyá, she is your daughter. Protect her always for me always, Yemanyá." Then you turned towards me: "Yemanyá agrees but says you must never cut your hair." Yemanyá demanded long hair, and you did too—the Goddess because of an ancestral rite, and you because it excited you in lovemaking. My God, how my long hair excited you.

You told me about Brazil; you told me that in Bahía the wise men had initiated you with chicken blood and that you had always liked living among blacks.

I knew at once that it was the happiest day of my life.

In a gesture full of social sound and fury, you broke with your past. And we sealed our union in that sea, the most beautiful place on earth.

The most beautiful place on earth belonged to the blacks and the indians. It was called Talamanca.

"Señor, could you tell me why no one answers in the Wildlife Office? I need some information about the Gandoca Wildlife Refuge."

"Oh, listen, that's run by the Park System now."

"How strange! The Wildlife Office isn't in charge of wildlife sanctuaries?"

The Ministry employee shrugged his shoulders. I thanked him and left.

"Is this the Legal Department of the Park System?"

"That's right. What can I do for you, Señora?

"Are you in charge of the Gandoca Wildlife Refuge?"

"Yes."

"Why? The Refuges aren't Parks."

"It was a high-level administrative decision. I can't explain it to you."

"But did they change the laws on refuges so that the Park System manages them now?"

"No, I don't think so."

"Could you give me a copy of the bylaws and regulations that apply in the Gandoca Refuge?"

"Ummmm. . . wait. I'll find out. Sit down, please; have a seat."

The lawyer left the office. I leaned back in the chair and sighed. After a while, he popped his head in and said, "Give me a second; I can't find them." I waited nearly half an hour longer. He came back with another official, who was very young.

"Look, unfortunately, we don't have the bylaws in this office."

"Okay, but is there someone who can explain to me what changes have occurred in the regulations? The reason I'm asking is that it used to be difficult to get permission from the Manager of the Refuge even to build a little shack there, but now trees are chopped down everyday, and hotels and cabins pop up everywhere without rhyme or reason, all of which dump sewage and garbage onto the beaches and into the rivers."

"I'm going to ask the Head of the Legal Department."

They both walked out and left me alone in the office.

After a while, the lawyer returned without the young official.

"I'm afraid the Head of the Legal Department says that the regulations have not been changed at all."

"If the regulations are the same, then why isn't anyone following them?"

"That's because much of the refuge is on private property."

"I know, but the owners have known for many years that all private property there has certain restrictions in order to protect the wildlife."

"No. Private property is private property. It can't be restricted."

"But it can be regulated! For example, suppose that I have a lot in a residential neighborhood, and I decide to build a nuclear plant on it. Obviously, they wouldn't let me."

"Well, they very well may have to let you. Private property rules."

"Okay, some other day you can explain that to me. But for now I just want to see the bylaws of the Gandoca sanctuary."

"Ask in the Wildlife Office. I've already told you that we don't have them in the Legal Department."

"And I already told you that there's no one in the Wildlife Office."

"Go and see for yourself; the office isn't far from here."

At that moment, the younger official entered, took me discreetly by the arm, and said in a low voice, "Why don't you do something: put all of these questions in writing to the Director of the Park System."

The bylaws and regulations didn't show up in the Wildlife Office. After an hour, a friendly guy found them and gave them to me, saying, "Xerox them, and give them back to me."

The bylaws stated that the primary purpose of the Gandoca Refuge was to protect wildlife and that anyone interested in developing a tourist business should present an environmental impact study. However, they didn't say anything about the kind of tourism to be developed. Was it tacitly assumed that such tourism should not violate the main purpose of the Refuge, which is to preserve wildlife? For that matter, what exactly *is* wildlife? Does it encompass the golden sand and living fossils? The dizzying odor of wild lilies? The silence at five o'clock in the morning just before the birds sing? The silence of the night?

I got home anxious and confused.

The dawn is just about to break. I know that because of the bird, which begins "tit . . . tit . . . tit . . . tit . . . tit tit tit," like a machine getting warmed up, and when it is going at full power, it stops abruptly and says, "ffeeuuu, ffeeuuu, ffeeuuu." The bird does that just at daybreak. It's getting light. I get up from my bed and go.

I like to go outside in the morning because it's like the first day of creation; the expanse of water and the expanse of sky are just separating. The blue herons wash their feet. The sea is as warm as the sheets I have just left, as warm as your arms. It is the warm and wild sea of the Gandoca Refuge, full of red sponges and fiery corals.

You brought me here. You carried me off, Carlos Manuel, to give me a complete lesson on love and on the spiritual function of light. I had loved the rain and the jungle from childhood. You taught me that there is jungle at the bottom of the sea and that it also rains there.

What's I am experiencing now is therefore all your fault: you showed me the meaning of love and beauty and then left me all alone—alone walking barefoot toward Chiquita Beach and gathering the white exoskeleton of the sea urchins. The waves are breaking loudly on the horizon, and the water is acquiring the texture of burnished glass as the sun rises. I pause to daydream in the humidity of the sea grape and blue mahoe trees. You brought me here and then left me talking by myself among the *saragundí* trees.

I wrote a brief letter to the Parks Director. The Director never answered me but sent word by way of another official: "With respect to the Gandoca Refuge, you should talk with Sergei Domeniev. Here's the number; take it." I didn't then know that civil servants are required by law to answer in writing. I wasn't aware of my rights as a citizen, and I simply accepted the Director's verbal response.

It was torture to hunt for the famous Sergei, for he was never available, and he did not deign to return my calls. When I finally reached him by phone, he said, "What is happening is serious. Come to my office and I'll show you."

It was an office of the Organization of American States. "What does the OAS have to do with the Refuge?" I asked him.

"I'm the Regional Director of the Biosphere Reserve, a binational project of the OAS between Panama and Costa Rica. The Park System asked us to help run the Gandoca Refuge because it is now part of the Biosphere Reserve, declared a World Heritage Site by UNESCO."

"The Gandoca Refuge is now a World Heritage Site?"

"In effect."

"Look, Sergei, you don't need to convince me that serious things are happening in this World Heritage Site. Right behind my cottage on Punta Uva, a French woman has all of a sudden decided to build sixteen cabins, a restaurant, and a *discothèque*. On one side of her are Don Wallis Black's eight cabins, and next to him, another investor is building twenty cabins. Another company plans to build forty in front, and next to those a Canadian investor wants to build a 200-room hotel. All of this in a diameter of 800 meters. With so many people there, the wildlife is going to be run off."

"That's nothing compared to what's already in the works here. Look at this hotel, which will also be on Punta Uva."

Sergei laid the blueprints on his desk.

I observed the blueprints carefully, and I asked him to give me a copy of all of the related documents he had. He gave them to me and let me study them without interruption.

When I finished, I exclaimed with surprise, "This project isn't a hotel; it's a residential development! Look, it has sixty lots, streets, and condominiums. There's even a shopping center, a beauty salon, a cafeteria, a couple of dance clubs, and what looks like a skating rink, not to mention ninety bungalows, tennis courts, and look at this . . . I don't know why, but I suspect that the rink is for ice-skating. In other words, this place is going to be a mini-Miami!"

Sergei shrugged his shoulders, muttering, "They've proposed it as a hotel."

"Who are 'they'?"

"The 'Ecodollars' Company, Inc.—some Italians. The architect and the engineers of the project are powerful, high-society Costa Ricans. No one can stop them. They've met all of the requirements."

"Which requirements?"

"The ones that the Gandoca Refuge Regulations stipulate for touristic development. The only thing missing is the environmental impact study."

"If the environmental impact study is missing, how can you tell me that they have met all of the requirements?"

I rushed to talk to a lawyer. He explained that, according to the Shoreline Zone Law, in order to grant concessions and build hotels on a tourist beach, it was necessary to have a Management Plan in place. This Management Plan established what, where, how, and how much could be constructed. But according to an interpretation of Article 73, that law did not apply to the beaches of the Refuge, for which reason the requirement of a Management Plan did not apply either. I told him that the beaches of the sanctuaries were, of course, excluded with the understanding that distinct and probably more severe or extensive regulations applied there. He said that of course they were but that that was merely my deduction, for the law didn't actually say so anywhere, and because of that, there was no legal obligation.

I said, "It's not an obligation according to the letter of the law, but it is an obligation according to the spirit of the law—isn't it?"

He shrugged his shoulders.

"And the wildlife?" I asked him.

The lawyer shrugged his shoulders again.

And the wildlife? The marine turtles that depend on the sea pastures? The mangroves? The sponges of every color, the algae? The intoxicating odor of the flowers at sunset? The beach morning glories, the lilies, the soursops, the Raphia palms, the marshes, the *cativos*, the cawi trees, the cedars, the orchids, the peccaries, the large anteaters, the manatees? The creeks that flow into the sea by way of a different mouth each time it rains?

My oldest son is on the lookout for the manatee just like they await the famous Loch Ness monster in Scotland; that's why he adores getting into the rivers of the Refuge. Those rivers are called creeks in *mecaitelia*, the local dialect. In Ernesto Creek, a man with a bare ass is defecating in the clear, beautiful water. He is defecating in the water in which minutes earlier my son was swimming. His immense cheeks are exposed to the sight and patience of anyone passing by. The loose excrement falls into the transparent waters of Ernesto Creek. Offended, my son turns his face away. I keep watching. The man has a roll of toilet paper. He unrolls a bit and cleans himself well. He tosses the dirty paper into the marvelous waters of Ernesto Creek. He wipes himself several times. He keeps throwing bunches of paper full of shit into the creek. When a change of breeze wafts the stench my way, I tell my son, "Let's get out of here!"

The Minister was a former manager of Chunchi Cola, but the Vice-Minister had been a famous conservationist, one of the founders of the park system. It was with great difficulty that I obtained an appointment. After a month, he granted me a five-minute interview. I said—without breathing so that I could fit as much as I could into the five minutes—, "Señor Vice-Minister, I am deeply grieved because the investors are destroying that area. How is it possible that in a Wildlife Refuge there is no regulation telling people how to build? How is it possible that an area that is not legally protected requires a management plan while a protected area requires *none at all*?" The Vice-Minister looked at his watch, nodded his head, lifted his hand, and said, "They've told me that that Refuge is already too far gone, that it's not even worth protecting anymore. A pleasure, señora, adios."

It's not even worth protecting anymore. My secret passion is to walk at morning through the jungle while it is sunk in humidity and in silence. The rain has shifted the sand, the rivers, the rocks, the trees, and the stones. The green flowers of the forest float into the sea.

I go into the sea for the flowers, submerging myself slowly into a mute, radiant world. But I feel dangerously light-headed, because I left before breakfast and am snorkeling on an empty stomach. I am already far from shore and weak. I humbly announce to the Lady of the Atlantic that I have not cut my hair, which is now fully and undulantly extended in her lap. Exhausted, I give myself up to the rocking, pushing waves that carry me, like everything else that drifts on this sea, toward the beach.

I have been deposited limp and exhausted on the golden sand. A group of howler monkeys descends from the trees to look at me. The one that watches me the most is a female monkey. She rubs her belly a lot; she's pregnant. I get up and begin to walk slowly. A family has driven up to the sand in a camper. The father of the family takes out his machete and methodically cuts four, five, six sea grape trees and then begins to slash a coco plum. "Hey, Señor, this is a Wildlife Refuge; what are you doing?"

"Don't mess with me, you madwoman!" he answers, threatening me with his machete. His wife watches him with approval and keeps unrolling a tent. The man now attacks a blue mahoe tree. Then he and his wife set aside the trimmed branches, the trunks, the fallen trees. I forget that I'm weak, and I stay there watching them. In the cleared area, they set up the tent and make a fire. Two children come out of the camper. "The place isn't even worth protecting anymore," said the Vice-Minister.

I wrote the Vice-Minister to declare that, in my opinion, the Gandoca Refuge was still a sanctuary and that it should be protected for all posterity. I said that if they wanted to develop it for tourism instead, then they needed to plan accordingly, because allowing unplanned development would simply ruin it. I stated that urbanization would also kill it and that the plans presented by the Italians were very clear in their intent to cut the entire jungle, dry it out completely, and build. I added that I had carefully studied the prevailing laws and had found out that the Ministry was now violating Article 2 of the Forestry Law, Article 18 of the Wildlife Law, Articles 9 and 10 of the Refuge Regulation Act, and Article 1 of the Refuge Creation Act.

My letter to the Vice-Minister was full of passion and common sense.

Because of that letter, she—the woman with the hoarse and peremptory voice—called me. She, Ana Luisa. I don't know why, but when I saw her, I thought her name should be French: *Anne Louise*. And when she smiled, I thought that her charm lay in her irregular teeth, *ses dents bousculées*.

"Your letter to the Vice-Minister is excellent, and I'm going to help you. First, you have to contact the eminent biologist Alvaro Cienfuegos. His scientific authority is unquestionable. If he provides us with the technical criteria to defend the resources of the Refuge, the Vice-Minister has to defend them."

"What should I do?"

"I have given you a project within my Program for Protection of Endangered Species. It may sound to you like a soccer game, but it's called 'Defense of the Gandoca Refuge.'"

"Thanks, Ana Luisa."

"Don't mention it; it's in the national interest. Do you like the sea a lot?"

"I like it very much. Especially *that* sea."

There are smooth seas of a uniform indigo blue and perfect seas like the Pacific Ocean. There are seas with twenty meters of transparency, like the Caribbean at San Blas. The sea of the Gandoca Refuge is a different thing altogether.

It's not a snorkeling sea because it is turbulent ten months a year. It's not blue; it has a changing spirit, now green, now violet, now grey. It can't be offered to the traditional tourist who measures the success of a vacation by the color of his or her tan, because it is often overcast and rainy. I am well acquainted with it, and I know that it is not a sea but rather an interior place, a temperament, an important stage in self-awareness. To sit on the beaches of the Gandoca Refuge is to transcend everything, including its own proper arbitrary beauty—its eternally perfumed but decaying flowers and algae.

You brought me to this sea, Carlos Manuel, so that I could hear the rising voice of its birds and waves and see the tortoises grazing in the afternoon. We sank up to our ankles in the mud and labored through the unsteady footing of the marsh to get to the beach and to our lot. We built our cottage discretely, carrying the materials on our shoulders and cutting and destroying as little as possible. You sat with Wallis Black to add up the costs, including not only the wood but also its transportation on the back of Paco, the burro. You began to build the hut with Wallis's brother Owen. You always got along well with them. I only learned too late that you felt like them: segregated, black, dissident, and rejected by high society. I saw only too late that beneath the proud names of your ancestry lurked an unhappy, marginalized, evasive black man who tended to drown his sorrows in alcohol. You always got along well with them, and for many years I asked myself no questions. For many years, I simply observed with pride that you were attached to the life of these autarchic fishing communities, which peacefully coexisted with the wilderness.

I did not realize until too late that we were both connected to that land of blacks for different, almost opposing reasons.

The Gandoca Refuge was a perfect site, our sacred site; thus, the beauty it gave us had to be eternal, like our love.

I entered the Institute of Ocean Sciences. I had an appointment with Alvaro Cienfuegos, the country's foremost coral reef specialist. Alvaro was a slender man of few words.

"Good morning, Alvaro, let me introduce myself. My name is Daniela Zermat, and I work for the Ministry on a project called Defense of the Gandoca Refuge. My boss is Ana Luisa, the Director of the Endangered Species Program. She told me that you have studied the coral reefs of the Refuge extensively and are well acquainted with their value."

"It's nice to meet you. Come in. Yes, the reefs of Gandoca are unique; they're really extraordinary. We scientists are only just beginning to study them, and we're already amazed by the biodiversity they contain."

"But in the Ministry they're saying that the Refuge isn't worth protecting anymore."

"What? They're crazy!"

"Furthermore, they're going ahead with urban development plans that will require cutting down all of the trees."

"But the Ministry knows that trees are essential to the protection of a reef. Tell me again: what do they want to do?"

"They want to promote urban development in the Refuge. They're already leveling seaside properties to build a bunch of cabins without rhyme or reason."

"Yes, we biologists were worried by the acceleration of informal activities that lately . . ."

"They're informal because the Ministry now refuses to exercise even minimal controls."

"Of course, we biologists were worried because we don't see any controls. Why don't they exercise them?"

"They say they can't because there is private property in the Refuge."

"There has always been private property there, but they used to regulate its use."

"Now the owners are of a different kind. Perhaps they don't want to control them because of that."

"Yes, we've seen a lot of expensive cars coming to the beaches lately."

"Besides, they move the administration of the Refuge from one office to another: they took it away from Wildlife to give it to Parks. Now Parks has given it to Biosphere Reserve. And we'll go there right now, Alvaro, if you'll allow me."

I took the VIP's arm and escorted him to Sergei's office. I showed him the "Ecodollars" Company blueprints. He examined them slowly with me. The more documents he examined, the more his face darkened.

Alvaro returned sadly to the Institute, thinking about the scientific letters that he was going to send. I asked Sergei to lend me the "Ecodollars" Company blueprints—public documents—and I went to copy them. I was on my way back to the Office of the Organization of American States with the load of blueprints under my arm when a young man—he introduced himself as a legal assessor of Wildlife—announced that he had come by order of the Minister to take back all of the records of the Gandoca Refuge. The Minister had claimed that those records had nothing to do with an international office. Visibly upset, Sergei tried to stop him.

"Señor, the Refuge is part of the Biosphere Reserve; that's why the OAS . . ."

"I don't know anything about that; I only know that the Minister has ordered it all to be transferred back to the Wildlife Office, as the law states."

I handed over the original plans to the lawyer. He took his leave after loading the records in the arms of an assistant, who almost fainted under the weight but docilely followed him, panting heavily.

Sergei and I remained stupefied. After a while he reacted, exclaiming, "I wonder what they're hiding behind all of this."

"In the Ministry they don't want to defend the Gandoca Refuge. They want to hand it over to investors. They even have you convinced."

"Convinced of what?"

"That it's impossible to stop the Italians; that was your initial comment when you showed me the blueprints for the first time."

"Yes, it's true. I think it will be very difficult to stop them."

"Fortunately, Ana Luisa convinced the Vice-Minister to give me a chance."

"And what's that wonderful chance that the Vice-Minister has given you?" he asked sarcastically.

"To gather technical studies that show the biological value of the site. With those documents in his hands, the Vice-Minister—according to Ana Luisa— can defend it or at least plan the development accordingly."

"Technical studies have already been done."

"The Vice-Minister does not consider them sufficient."

"Yet, the one who took the documents away was not the Vice-Minister but the Minister," murmured Sergei. "What does the Minister have to do with all of this?"

Wallis Black had seventeen brothers. Eighteen light-eyed Afro-Caribbeans. They say that they have regarded you highly for the last fifteen years, Carlos Manuel, ever since, as a practicing anthropologist, you came to work here and lived among them.

One of Wallis Black's older brothers is crouched on a trunk near the sea, carving it. I sit with the children to watch him cutting the wood. My oldest son discovers that he is making a boat. He remains for hours and hours to watch him work. From time to time, my son lifts his little head to observe the flying ospreys outlined against the sky.

Soon, the boat emerges from the tree trunk. The children ask Wallis's brother to let us go to the coral in the boat. It's a quiet and sweet summer.

It's a summer as sweet as a poppy. I like to get water from the well and carry it home in a bucket. I like not having electricity and, as a result, having to arrange our activities around the sun's schedule. We're immensely happy, Carlos Manuel, and excessive happiness is painful. I love you with a burning, intemperate love.

It's the dog days of July, and I walk with our children along the seashore collecting dry sea urchins to make a mobile while you are busy with Wallis doing things around the place. One of the children asks, "Where's Daddy?"

I remember that summer as the highest and most perfect point of all our years together. The cawi trees had bloomed, and the ground was full of yellow flowers. The beach morning glories had also bloomed, and a thick, multicolor carpet covered the sand. The orchids were opening on the coconut palms, and behind the beach but in front of the Raphia palms, a white multitude of wild irises perfumed the marine silence. Some blacks passed by, and their mules left round hoofprints in which the children stepped. Then we met with a retinue of non-

Spanish-speaking indians. I reflected that for centuries indians and blacks had maintained this shore intact. And at that moment I had the horrifying certainty, Carlos, that you, and I, and Wallis and his seventeen brothers—whose parents were born and lived and loved on this coast and baptized their wonders in *mecaitelia*—were poised right at the outset of its profanation.

I felt your mouth and the intoxicating aroma of the *ilang ilang* flower that you brought in your hand. You said, "For you." You murmured, "I love you."

"Not now, Carlos Manuel; the children are over there."

"In the sea, then."

The crystal sea changes like a kaleidoscope that always begins anew.

Ah, to lie down in the sea. The warm green beds of turtle grass.

To be penetrated to our innermost depths by the Caribbean Sea when love reaches the limits of the tropics in a green enchantment of stilled estuaries and palm trees that grow upside down.

Seated on your legs and rocked in your arms by the residual waves of passion, I dared to ask you, "How long is this going to last, Carlos?"

"Do you mean how long is our love going to last?"

"Yes, our love, our happiness, this perfect beach, the smell of wildflowers."

"It's going to last for ever, little Pale Face. When we're old, we'll come here to warm our bones. I promise and swear to you that I will be at your side until I die."

I sink into the green seaweed, into beds of sponges, into your hoarse, grave voice that continues to vibrate until a wave thunders over the reef and muffles it.

"Now you have to get some funding for your Refuge Defense project," Ana Luisa said to me, "funding to pay for the technical studies. There are five European countries that are donating a lot of money for conservation."

Armed with the new Ministry post given to me by Ana Luisa with the endorsement of the Vice-Minister, I am on my way to the embassy of one of the donating countries. I proudly present my project to defend the Gandoca Refuge. I am soliciting funding for the technical studies. The ambassador grants me an appointment.

He's a tall, blond, and nice man. I'm sitting in front of him in the anteroom of his office. In his hands are the Gandoca Refuge Regulations, which I sent him.

"It's a pleasure to meet you, Señora. So you work in the Ministry."

"Yes, Señor."

"And you want to protect the Gandoca Refuge."

"That's right."

"And you want our country to help you with funding."

"Yes, Señor, for the technical studies. If you can't provide funding, perhaps you could grant me scientific aid."

"Well, I'd like to know some things. This Act contains all of the technical reasons that justify the creation of that Refuge."

"That's correct."

"The Refuge was created six years ago on the basis of a series of scientific studies."

"Yes, Señor."

"Here is a list of the resources that are being protected by decree of its creation. Why is it necessary to do the studies all over again?"

"The Vice-Minister has requested it."

"But why? Does the Vice-Minister assume that the studies that gave rise to the creation of the Refuge were poorly done?"

"I don't think so. He probably fears that the resources have deteriorated excessively since the Refuge was created."

"And is that true?"

"Excessively, no. But they are deteriorating quickly. That's why I'm interested in protecting it now!"

"Hmmmm. . . . Okay, I'm going to study the project, and we'll let you know within a few weeks."

"I can't thank you enough, Señor Ambassador."

"Mama, did you see those awesome corals? There are red ones, orange ones. . ."

"Yes, my love, but don't go so far out. There are entrances in the reef through which the sharks come."

"Papa and I saw a white eagle manta ray with little black spots!"

"I saw a better one that was this big."

"I saw a drummer fish."

"I saw some blue ones, some purple ones, and some yellow ones with a false eye."

"The ones with the false eye are called angelfish."

We have snorkeled for hours on the reef. The sun shone without a cloud all day. Now the evening is falling, and the shadows advance across the sea. It's time to go home.

Night falls while we are walking across the sand. The night is thick, but its dark fabric is pinpricked as though by little holes. They are fireflies.

Their greenish glow illuminates the cottage so much that it is unnecessary to light candles.

But on that greenish-glowing night, I was anxiously awakened by a very sad song. The bird sang only twice, and that was enough to tear me apart. You also heard it, Carlos Manuel. Frightened, I asked you what bird it was. You said, "I don't know; I've never heard it before. It sounds like an emerald toucanet, but it isn't one."

It sang once more, crying as though it were complaining of some frightful pain.

I held you hard to shield myself against that bird's pain. I hugged you violently, hoping that you would hold me even harder, but you didn't move; you were already in a deep sleep.

When the investors came, Carlos Manuel, you and I were happy and untroubled. I thought that the administrators of the Refuge—the ones who had presented themselves at the building of our cottage, the ones who were entrusted with making sure that no one harmed the natural habitat—would put a halt to the strangers' designs.

The investors were people who hated the mud, the insects, the jungle, and the humidity. Even the blue carpet of the beach morning glories bothered them; all they wanted was the expanse of golden sand, which they coveted greatly. These people began to buy. After buying up the land, they drained it, because they hated the marshes. They spread pesticides because they hated every bug, every crab. They cleared the jungle because they wanted to make gardens instead. They cut down the trees at the edges of rivers to build platforms, so as not to dirty their feet.

There are many versions of how and why they came. Some say that it was inevitable because the rumor had spread that the beaches were perfect. So much beauty could not keep itself secret forever.

Others say that it was because of the road, without which the beauty would have remained hidden. Others say that it was because of the white man's avarice, and because the whites told the blacks patent lies: "Sell us your farms because they're inside the Refuge, and soon you won't be able to work them." Others— the more racist ones—simply say that blacks are like that: they'll sell everything because they like to get easy money and not have to work. Still others say that the blacks sold out because they were very poor and were happy to have cash and be able to go to the dentist for the first time. And, finally, others say that they sold out because the *monilia* disease attacked their cocoa crops and took away their sole income and means of subsistence.

The investors arrived at high speeds in incredibly luxurious vehicles, scaring people and animals. One could see them in the pensions of Puerto Viejo, drunk from expensive whiskey and shouting until morning. They annihilated the natural silence with their stereos at full blast, and they violated the voice of the sea with the deafening noise of their dirt bikes on the beach.

I was certain that the Refuge administrators would stop them.

When I realized that the owners of the BMWs, Range Rovers, and Mercedes kept on buying, cutting, draining, and dumping tons of crab-killing pesticides without anyone restraining them, and especially when the electricity arrived, and rumors spread that they were going to pave the road, it was too late: I was already absorbed in your affairs, Carlos Manuel, utterly closed off to the world and dizzily clinging to what remained of your love and of yourself, trying to save both.

It was a strange coincidence that the bells of the Refuge's destruction and the bells of your illness sounded the alarm at the same time. That's why I didn't even realize that the bells of the Refuge were sounding the alarm. I was desperate, and all I could hear was the sound of your destruction pounding in my head.

The Ambassador scheduled an appointment quickly. I arrived with enthusiasm and high hopes.

"You know, Doña Daniela, that our government has contributed a lot of money to this country for conservation. Much of this money has been wasted. Now we are stricter in donating. We study more carefully whether or not the donation we make will serve some purpose. In the past, political motives have obstructed the course of technical studies, for which reason the funding for technical studies was wasted. From now on, our government wants to be sure that the technical effort that it is helping to finance will be politically viable, so that the money and the effort are not wasted. Do you understand?

"Of course, Señor."

"We are aware that great economic pressures weigh on the Gandoca Refuge."

"Of course they do, Señor Ambassador; I already assumed that. That's why it's so urgent to carry out the technical studies."

"As you know, economic pressures are political pressures."

". . ."

"It's not possible for us to aid your Gandoca Refuge Defense Project because it is precisely one of those cases in which technical efforts will most probably be annulled by political pressures. You understand our position."

I felt very ashamed.

In the evening, I called Ana Luisa and told her the result of my dealings with the Embassy. After a long silence on the telephone, she told me not to lose heart.

The next day, she called to tell me that Alvaro Cienfuegos had sent the Vice-Minister various studies on the coral reefs of Gandoca, with a copy for me.

Alvaro's studies were almost poetical. They spoke of the fossil reefs, of the live reefs, of the sponges in their fragile and immense variety. They spoke of exceptional mollusks and mentioned, for example, that ninety percent of the sixty new species of algae discovered in our country were from the Refuge.

I asked Ana Luisa what the Vice-Minister had thought of the studies. In my opinion, they were more than enough to defend the site against wind and tide. She told me that the Vice-Minister had not said anything.

Days passed, I wasn't getting the funding I sought for the technical studies, and the Vice-Minister wasn't accepting the scientific studies that Alvaro had sent him.

"I don't understand," I said desperately to Ana Luisa. The Vice-Minister asks for technical studies, and when I give them to him, he doesn't take them into account. What does he want, then?"

"He thinks it isn't enough yet. He says that you should ask Alvaro Cienfuegos for a proposal to do a technical study and then find a way to pay him for it.

On Punta Uva, Carlos Manuel, I encountered the bitter truth of your love and the end of the magic spell.

In your painstaking effort to avoid polluting the environment, you wanted to improve the septic tank as the sanitary engineer had recommended. Obsessively, you insisted on going to do this job immediately. I accompanied you without the children.

On Sunday morning you finished the shoveling and started to drink beer. You had always liked beer, and I had never seen anything abnormal about this.

But when I saw you drink the tenth one before twelve o'clock, my body began to bristle like the back of a menaced dog.

You were frightfully drunk. I had never seen you like that. Thick and pasty-tongued, you said that it was a disgrace that I was such a moderate drinker and so utterly un-bohemian. I answered, "You're no bohemian either." You shouted that you were and that you had made an effort to hide it from me throughout all of these years because you were afraid to disappoint me. But that you couldn't pretend anymore.

I answered that it was no disgrace and that I could accept you no matter how different your tastes were. Your bleary golden-green eyes glared defiantly as you opened another beer.

I tried not to give the matter any importance. I got the suitcases ready, tidied up the house, and collected the tools. When everything was ready, I looked for the car keys. I didn't find them. You had them, and you laughed loudly, letting me know that you weren't going to let me drive. When I tried to take the key chain, you grabbed the staircase railing and gave me a kick in the belly—the belly that had borne your children. I fell breathless, and you took advantage of my fall to beat me on the face and breast. When I got up, you tried to knock me down again with the bottle. But you were too drunk, and you missed the target. I fled. The horror of that afternoon still reverberates in my head.

Upon arriving at the capital, I called your doctor, and then I called your brother.

The three of us are seated in the doctor's office. "What's wrong with Carlos Manuel?" I ask. Your brother looks at the wall, saying nothing. The doctor asks me to describe in detail what has happened. "He turned into a murderer," I say shamefully, and I burst into tears.

Finally your brother speaks with the voice of the living dead: "Carlos Manuel was an alcoholic. I say 'was' because we all believed that he had been cured."

"He loves you so much," interrupted the doctor. "Sometimes love can work miracles. We all believed that love had cured him."

The horror of that afternoon still reverberates in my head. For me, that afternoon put an end to beauty, bounty, and tenderness. The giant almond trees, the carpets of beach morning glories, and the warm green beds of turtle grass—all ceased to occupy an important place in my life. The core of my life became the struggle against your nightly rambling, your violence, your unending drinking.

Alvaro Cienfuegos and two other eminent biologists wrote an urgent study proposal. I called Ana Luisa to tell her.

"Don't get too happy, Daniela. The Wildlife Office just approved the 'Ecodollars' Company hotel."

"The urban development? But how could they do so without a Management Plan, without an environmental study, without any planning whatsoever. . ."

"Because it is private property, Daniela; get it into your head that they have a title deed to the property."

"But it's a public shoreline zone restricted by law."

"They moved the project to just behind the shoreline zone."

"That's the shoreline impact area."

"But they have the title deed to the property."

"Still, Wildlife's approval is against the law and the regulations."

"In order to apply the law, we would have to indemnify them."

"I can't believe that, Ana Luisa."

I desperately called the lawyer again, who assured me that the decision could be challenged. He gave me the name of an environmental lawyer.

Mariana was blond, suave, and very bright. I explained the case, and she agreed that we should fight it. She advised me to begin by explaining the situation to the Attorney General for the Environment.

I wrote a very detailed letter to the Attorney General for the Environment asking his opinion and requesting his advice. Meanwhile, I presented the proposal by Alvaro Cienfuegos and the other University biologists to the Vice-Minister. I asked Ana Luisa, "What does the Vice-Minister say of the 'Ecodollars' urban development?"

"Does the Vice-Minister realize that to build this urban development it will be necessary to cut down all, *absolutely every single one*, of the trees on the property? Does the Vice-minister know that if 'Ecodollars' is permitted to cut down all of the trees on their property, the same thing will have to be permitted on every property? Is the Vice-Minister aware that European investors love to pave over everything? Does the Vice-Minister realize that we thereby run the legal risk of leaving *not one single tree* in that Refuge?"

"It wasn't the Vice-Minister who gave the approval to that project, Daniela. It was the Wildlife Office."

I went to speak to the head of Wildlife. One word sounded obsessively in my head: chicanery. It sounded so loudly that perhaps the head of Wildlife heard it, because after much begging on my part, he agreed to receive me. He was an older man—humble, timid, scared. The lawyer who had taken the documents from the OAS office came to support him. He told me that I had no reason to stick my nose in, that they were the ones in charge, that everyone in the Ministry was *sick* of me, that I should stop bothering them *now*, that this was a case of private property, and that he didn't want the justices of the Constitutional Tribunal to take away his car."

"Why are they going to take away your car?"

"To indemnify the investors for losses and damages; don't you see that it is private property?—the state shouldn't stick its nose in <u>anything</u>."

"Who decided that?"

"The Constitutional Tribunal."

"But it's also illegal to approve the 'Ecodollars' project," I said. The Refuge Regulations require investors to prepare an environmental impact statement. They haven't prepared it."

"It appears that they have," intervened the director.

"That's not true. Have you seen it, Señor Director? Have you studied it? Evaluated it?"

The head of the Wildlife Office was sweating. When he lifted the receiver to call the minister, his hands were shaking.

The man was pitiful. I left.

"Ana Luisa, the studies requested by the Vice-Minister have to be started *now*. The biologists' proposals have to be approved as soon as possible."

"Yes, Daniela. But please leave your worries this afternoon, get ready, and come with me to the celebration of Earth Day at the Presidential House." Ana Luisa glowed with middle-aged seductiveness. The Vice-Minister was making the most of his handsome physique and looked like a movie star in spite of his crooked nose. There I met the Head of the System of Parks Legal Department, a plump and pleasant woman lawyer.

The President of the Republic proclaimed and repeated that one of his priorities was environmental protection and that he was proposing the creation of a New International Ecological Order to Costa Rica and to the world.

I couldn't help feeling hopeful upon hearing him.

Then the Minister spoke. He said in a tremulous voice that the riches of our country were the forests, that he was going to create two new parks along the

Northern Pacific shore, and that he remained committed to caring for the natural resources of Costa Rica. When he finished speaking, I felt happy. Here I was suffering for the Gandoca Refuge, and nobody had informed me that the Minister was my ally. I ran over to talk to him.

He also looked relaxed and content. He held a glass in his hand.

"Señor Minister," I said with deep emotion, "what a great speech! You must help me with the Gandoca Refuge. I'm Daniela Zermat."

"It's a pleasure, Daniela. We're already aiding the Gandoca Refuge by bringing progress to it. I am just about to approve a hotel there."

"Señor Minister, you can't approve any hotel without a management plan."

"But it's a little hotel. What harm could it do?"

"It's an urban development with dance clubs, thousands of streets, thousands of condominiums . . ."

"No, no, it's just a small hotel with two hundred rooms. Beautiful."

"The 'Ecodollars' hotel?"

"Of course, totally ecological. Daniela, look, there's nothing to be upset about."

"No, Señor Minister, you haven't looked at the blueprints carefully. They're going to build an ice-skating rink, several dance clubs, tennis courts, and thousands of gravel-filled lots without any trees. Besides, one has to look at the general problem of that area. The blacks will change from being owners to servants. That's not progress."

"Look, Daniela, just between you and me, what kind of work are you going to get blacks to do if not menial work?"

"But it isn't just the 'Ecodollars' project. There are thousands of others waiting until 'Ecodollars' gets permission. 'Ecodollars' is the tip of the spear. You have to act responsibly about that Refuge, Señor Minister."

Behind me, I heard Margarita, the Head of the Legal Department of the Parks System, the plump, pleasant one, saying, "That Daniela Zermat is truly a sweetheart and she's lovely today, but she's getting out of line with the Minister."

Margarita intervened and tried to take me with her so that I would leave the Minister alone, who was saying that he couldn't protect the Refuge because the Constitutional Tribunal had unfortunately ruled in favor of private property and against conservation, and he didn't want to have a lawsuit slapped on him.

"You're going to fail to fulfill your obligation because of fear? That's not ethical. Señor Minister, do you know the meaning of the word 'deontology'?"

I will never, ever, forget the look that the Minister gave me when he said, "I'm going to approve that little hotel, and you had better not judge the decisions of a Minister if you want to keep working in the Ministry."

As I am putting on my pajamas that evening, I reflect. Latin America is a land of tyrants. The tyrants characteristically say, for instance, that a green object is blue and that anyone who doesn't see the color blue gets punished. The "Ecodollars" Company submits the blueprints of an urban development. The Minister says that the urban development doesn't exist, that it's a hotel. And he threatens to punish me if I keep saying what I see in the blueprints.

I also remember that when the Minister said that evening that blacks are good for nothing but menial labor, a black official of the United States was walking by.

Several days later Ana Luisa informed me that the Minister was very annoyed by my attitude and that my visit had also made the head of Wildlife very nervous. She added that the Minister's legal counsel had decided that in reality the administration of wildlife refuges belonged to the Forestry Office.

"They're going to move the administration of the Gandoca Refuge to another office *again*?"

"These are legal decisions, Daniela."

The Forestry Office is a very strange place. Anyone who goes in and asks to see the Director will be asked, "Which one?" because there is a permanent General Director instated by law, but the Minister by fiat has created another Director to have his own toady on hand. Therefore, anyone who goes in sees the familiar nameplate: General Director of the Forestry Office. And in the office next to his: General Assistant Director of the Forestry Office. But a bit further on, one will see a big new nameplate that says Head Director and beside that, another office with an equally big nameplate that says Assistant Head Director. And so nobody knows who is the boss.

There in Forestry I learned that the Minister had assigned the "Ecodollars" Company case to the Assistant Head, his own yes-man.

The seashore now fills me with anxiety. I agree to go there on vacation with you and the children, but I watch closely for the moment when you're going to escape. I keep watching your eyes in terror of seeing the restlessness form in your greenish-yellow iris. When you tell your children that you're going for a moment to Wallace's cantina to buy some soft drinks and that you'll be right back, I panic. Because, in fact, you go into town to drink, and you don't come back for several days. Our children ask, "What's happened to Papa?"

Papa is in a bad mood when he doesn't drink, and when he does drink, he either acts like a monster or else he leaves. My fear is greater on Punta Uva, because the area has changed; now everyone is building cabins, dance clubs, restaurants, and bars, and there are a thousand temptations. People drink a lot of alcohol. Alcohol acts on your brain like poison. Your doctor told me, "Carlos Manuel shouldn't try any alcohol, Daniela. He can't tolerate it; it drives him crazy. Daniela, the best thing you two can do is to separate."

"Doctor, I love him. You're asking me to give up happiness."

"But you're no longer happy, Daniela. You're in pain."

"You're right."

Today I have just finished making a decision that has cost me innumerable nights of crying with my pillow in my mouth so that the kids don't hear me—nights that you don't sleep at home because you're out partying. When you arrive, I tell you. I tell you that I want us to separate. I tell you, Carlos Manuel, that we can't go on together.

My dream of love falls to pieces. The man of my life disappears. In front of me, there is only an irritable addict, a sick man whom I still love desperately with all the strength and intensity of new love.

You have knelt. You ask me please to give you another opportunity, one last chance. You say that you're going to stop drinking and detoxify yourself so as not to lose us—your wife and your children. And because I love you desperately with all of the strength and intensity of new love, I believe what you say.

I talk with your psychiatrist about your detoxification treatment. I tell him that I am full of faith and hope. But the doctor remains silent, shakes his head, and at last says that there is little likelihood that you will be cured. He adds that even from before the time you started to drink, you were already carrying death inside you and that your love for me and the years when you almost didn't drink can be regarded as a respite, a miracle.

Your head is resting on my lap. Your whole body feverishly trembles. You don't want to leave me even for a minute. And I don't want to lose you—I can't lose you, because my happiness depends on you.

I ask my brother whether or not they know about your condition at the office.

"Daniela, Carlos is a brilliant man. We notice, for example, that his hands tremble like those of an old man. But his work has never been better."

I know what that costs you, and I know that you do it for the children and me. You go to work, and you return home exhausted. The smallest noise startles and exasperates you. I admonish the children to keep quiet and to leave you in peace.

The Constitutional Tribunal was created a few years ago to resolve matters of compatibility between the laws and our constitution, as well as matters that were formerly handled by other tribunals or by the Supreme Court itself. I ask Ana Luisa which decision of the Constitutional Tribunal is the one that they invoke all of the time in the Ministry, the one that doesn't allow placing limits on private property. Ana Luisa says that it is the terrible Arenal decision, in which the Tribunal ruled that the Costa Rican government could not meddle with private property even for the purpose of an important public project such as the proposed Arenal hydroelectric dam project without first indemnifying the owners, because private property is sacred. Ana Luisa adds that, according to that ruling, not even the Health Law can be applied to private property.

I'm leaving my office in the Ministry when I hear a loud cry. Just then a hand takes hold of my dress and drags me behind a door to hide me. It's the Parks lawyer Margarita, the plump, pleasant woman. Through a crack in the door's hinges I see the Minister with a face the color of crimson and a letter in his hand like a raised lance. He is yelling that Daniela Zermat is utterly mad, that he has a madwoman in his Ministry, and that he must get rid of her because she is totally conniving, bad, and disrespectful. After several minutes I realize that the letter that the Minister is carrying in his hand is a warning sent by the Attorney for the Environment.

After assuring myself that the furious Minister isn't anywhere near and that Margarita is giving him a glass of water to calm him down, I emerge from my hiding place. I go quickly to the Post Office to see if the Attorney for the Environment has sent me a copy of the letter that he has written to the Minister.

Yes, I have a copy.

"The Attorney for the Environment respectfully gives notice to the Honorable Minister that a Wildlife Refuge is a Sanctuary and that the 'Ecodollars' project doesn't seem to fit the ends and purpose of a Sanctuary. Indeed, the fact that article 73 eliminates the need for a Management Plan along with the Institute of Tourism's control of the beaches of the Refuge does not permit the Minister to grant himself the power to develop tourism instead of protecting the area's natural resources. In addition, the Management Plan should not restrict itself merely to the shoreline but needs to regulate the *whole* Refuge more strictly, and before authorizing any tourist or hotel project, the capacity of the Sanctuary should be studied—for example, its capacity to sustain the discharge of contaminants."

The discharge of contaminants. In the "Ecodollars" project alone, imagine the garbage, the shit, and the urine of two thousand persons in just under thirty acres.

I went immediately to see Mariana, the environmentalist lawyer. I asked her, "Do you understand why the Minister got so angry? What's behind the 'Ecodollars' project anyway?"

"Not behind, Daniela, but *in* the project."

We sat down to study the blueprints with a group of architects and economists of governmental institutions for tourism. "Look," said one of the architects whose specialty was tourism planning, "Daniela's right. This project isn't a hotel, and it isn't for tourism. Pardon me for saying so, but the hotel bungalows are a screen for the real business, which is real-estate speculation. That's why it's divided into stages. First, the European investors make the pool, the hotel bungalows, the restaurants, etc. Then when the tourists arrive, they sell them the lots. That's the real business. That's why the Minister denies that it is a housing development, but they will never submit the blueprints without the housing development because *those are the real profits they're after*. And once the marsh is totally sold, cemented, and destroyed, what's it to them? The land will be worth much more—a simple matter of surplus value—and all of the neighbors will also become rich by developing. That's the whole point of the affair. Daniela, since you have a home there, do you know how much the Italians paid for the land?" I told them that I wasn't exactly sure but that one of the Italians' neighbors had bought forty-two acres from a black man for seven hundred thousand colones, which is to say, they paid about seventeen thousand an acre, and now an acre costs eight to twelve hundred thousand colones. "There's the speculation for you," said the architect.

An economist said that he had studied the "Ecodollars" accounts by order of the Institute of Tourism and that the figures that the Italians gave for the hotel were inflated. They weren't real. Upon correcting the figures, one could see that the hotel, which is to say the bungalows, weren't profitable. "Of course," the architect added, "that proves what I was just saying: the real business is just the housing development."

"Besides," said another architect, "there is the issue of density. For ecotourism a density of ten or fifteen percent is recommended. The 'Ecodollars' project has a density of ninety-five percent."

"The density is the percentage of the property that is built and inhabited?" asked sweet Mariana.

"Yes," the architects answered in unison.

"Besides making a windfall selling the lots," said another economist, "they sell destruction and return to Europe with the wealth. As Daniela just pointed out, from an investment of forty thousand colones, they can make six or seven million. Then they walk off and leave the problem of urban pollution and the destruction of the Refuge to the Costa Ricans. And we'll be in a fix to figure out how to handle this."

Ana Luisa informs me that the Head of Wildlife is still nervous and that the Vice-Minister has called a meeting in his office to deal with the problem of the Gandoca Refuge. She tells me that I should attend.

In the center of the office sits the Assistant Head of Forestry, the Minister's yes-man. He is tall, strong, and leaning back in his chair, as if presiding over the meeting.

But I am the one who begins the meeting, explaining the goal of my project.

Then I pause and get ready to enumerate the exceptional riches of the sanctuary. The Minister's yes-man butts in and says in a powerful voice that it's an empty Refuge, as empty as a barnyard empty of plants and animals. I disagree. I ask Alvaro Cienfuegos to talk a little about the marvelous things that abound there. Alvaro talks in a low voice. The Minister's yes-man says yes, there are marine riches in that Refuge but only marine ones; only the sea is rich. He knows that Alvaro Cienfuegos is a scrupulous scientist whose ethics require him to restrict himself to his field, the ocean.

The Assistant Head declares that there's no need to spend money protecting the land of the Refuge because it's not worth it: he himself has traversed, surveyed, and observed it with a magnifying glass, and there aren't even plants or animals, just a few puddles, some patches of jungle, two or three little parakeets, and that's all. I raise my voice and ask him if he has any scientific authority for saying so. The Assistant Head makes an evasive reply. The Vice-Ministers and the other high functionaries say nothing. They all know that the Assistant Head has no scientific authority, but they remain silent.

The next day Ana Luisa informs me that the Minister wants me to stop working at the ministry. He has named a Commission to study the case of the Gandoca Refuge, and, of course, I am not on it.

But Alvaro Cienfuegos is on it, because he is a marine biologist, and the sea is the only thing that's worth anything there.

But I, who have loved the Refuge so much and have traversed all of its forests even in my sleep, cannot accept that verdict. I call the Director of the Institute for the Study of Flora, a young scientist.

"Daniela, I can't believe what you're telling me! Look, this has got to be a case of bad faith. The Vice-Minister knows that the land portion of the Gandoca Refuge has been the biological corridor for the transmigration of species between North and South America. It's the site that contains the highest biodiversity in the lowlands of the Atlantic—that's why it was declared a Refuge. But just in case the Vice-Minister has a short memory, I will send him a summary as a reminder."

"You had better send it to the Minister."

"What's a former manager of Chunchi Cola going to understand about biodiversity? Better the Vice-Minister."

On the day that the summary from the Institute for the Study of Flora was ready, I got into bed early with the document and a bowl of fruit. The kids came to watch me out of curiosity. "It's seven o'clock, Mommy; why are you in bed already?"

"Because I'm reading something very exciting. Listen to this, kids: these forests around our cottage 'maintain a wealth of the most promising germplasm for the genetic improvement of traditional crops and for biochemical research in the area of health, natural pesticides, etc. The reserve supplies primary resources with which our ancestors met their needs. . . .'"

"What's 'germplasm'?" the oldest one asked.

48

"The source of life. The possibility that plants have of making other plants."

"Like the sperm and the ovule?"

"Yes, like the sperm and the ovule but without that. It's renewal."

"Our cottage is in a fantastic place?" asked the middle child.

"That's right."

"The snorkeling is what I like."

"I mother vegetables: my hog plum trees, *cativos*, kasha, and *guácimos* have all sprouted baby plants. But I want the jungle here, not a garden. That's one reason I have never killed the crabs, for they are like municipal garbage collectors. Crabs are, of course, big and bold. They go into houses and carry off the bread, toothbrushes, or matchboxes. That's why one has to leave everything carefully stowed away. The crabs are as big as cats, but I can't bring myself to grab them and cook them in a soup.

That was your favorite dish, Carlos. Blue crab soup.

I walk through the patio, intoxicated by the incredible aroma of monkey fruit tree flowers. While doing this, I hear men's voices behind me. How embarrassing—I'm in pajamas.

I run in to change, yelling, "I'll be right there."

It's Robinson, a mulatto, the former manager of the Refuge. He is with another man, whom he introduces to me as the schoolteacher of the fisherman's village. The teacher is worried, because a squatter has sold the trees at the springs for lumber, thereby endangering the water supply. Robinson has told him about my project in the ministry, and the teacher wants to know what's cooking in the capital. I tell him very sadly that in the ministry, they think that this unusual place, this migratory corridor of species, is a big empty lot that is good for nothing but urban development. Besides, the Minister has let me know that if I keep defending the flora, I'll lose my position at the Ministry.

The sea moans.

The teacher explains that the communities in the Refuge are unreliable and that the government has treated them very badly. The government only remembers that the blacks exist when it wants either their votes or their lands. It's even worse with the indians; since they don't vote or understand Spanish, the government doesn't even have to bother to lie to them.

He says that the communities in the Refuge can be wonderful but also terribly treacherous. They are fragmented and lack unity, but they have to be informed of what's going on.

"Why are you sad? Some memory just flitted across your eyes—were you thinking of your husband?" asks Ana Luisa.

"Yes. *It's the story of a love like no other, which made me understand everything good and everything evil.*[2] I went from sweet daily adoration to the very bottom of hell. For the evil began to filter through after several years of paradise, when my hands and feet were already tied by the cords of a binding love. 'Bitch!' he shouted irately. 'Treacherous bitch!' Yes, I was a bitch; he was right, although not in the sense that he had meant but rather in the sense of a female animal who was permanently in heat for him, constantly scenting his armpits. *Everything evil.* The ethylic poisons, the alkaloids—Carlos was even ready to rub toads to get them to eject their hallucinogenic milk so that he could drink it. At first, I wasn't aware in spite of the symptoms, for if you've never been with an addict before, how would you know? The first symptom was the high pulse rate, later the sour taste in his mouth, and then a substance that numbed my tongue when I kissed him. Something's wrong with you, I said: go and see a doctor; it's not normal; I'm afraid to kiss you. And he said, 'It's nothing, nothing at all; perhaps I drank too much coffee today at work.' He couldn't sleep, and he made love to me five or six times a night, even more than at the beginning. That and the sour taste would have been a dead giveaway to any woman who was either more cautious or less in love than I was. I didn't suspect anything at first,

---

[2] Lyrics from a popular bolero. [Tr.]

but for someone to caress, say sweet things, and make love continually to you all night long is normal at twenty, even at thirty, but not at forty without the help of some chemical substance. I should have put two and two together, but no, I just said, 'How delightful, how wonderful,' and sometimes, 'Let me sleep. I'm too tired.'"

"And the other side of the coin was the loneliness. The long nights of waiting while he, an aged adolescent, had fun partying at the bars. I can date the beginning of hell as the itching in his blood, the impossibility for him to return home early, the alkaloids making his kisses bitter, the liquor he consumed like water, and then the decline at dawn: his dirty pants; his shirttails hanging out; his glassy gaze; the children watching him with their backs against the wall, ashamed; the crying that spread by order of size, like the clanging of cowbells. Dragging his feet across the floor, he directed himself toward his room without looking at them and then shut the door and locked it. I remained behind, knowing that he was looking for the pistol and beginning the dance that we had seen enacted in the movie *Colonel Redl* by the incredible actor Jean Marie Brandauer before Carlos Manuel began drinking again—had he ever really stopped?—, but he had told me, 'That's the way I will try to kill myself.' Six years later I recalled the scene in the movie: the colonel dancing with the barrel of the pistol held tightly against his temple and the absolute desperation in his face. The only difference was that Carlos Manuel wasn't dancing but only tottering at best."

Ana Luisa looks shocked. She doesn't understand this sudden vomiting forth of intimate confidences. I see then that our friendship is still too fragile and cannot withstand it. I have frightened her, and the last thing I want now is for this new friendship to dry up. So I ask her pardon, I put tape over my mouth, and I leave.

You lay your head on my lap and try to listen to one of your favorite jazz records by Jacque Laroussier. But your perception is raw, and the quick, sharp notes irritate your soul. I get up, take off the record, and propose a substitute such as valium for the awful withdrawal symptoms. You don't want any. You grab my waist like a man who is in water up to his neck.

I no longer have the patience I had at the beginning: this is your third detoxification. The first two didn't work.

You put your head on my lap again. I am thinking that this is your last chance. If it doesn't work, I'm leaving.

I'll take my things out of the house. I'll take my things along with those of my children, and I will explain to them that you don't want to stop drinking and that the only solution left is to separate. I'll take them under my wing like little chicks, and with a broken soul, I will leave you.

They went up to my house and knocked on the door. They were the men from the various communities within the Refuge, a conjunction—unique in our country—of blacks, indians, and whites.

I was frightened. What did they want from me?

"Don't be afraid, little fawn; there's no reason to be," said the teacher. "The only thing we want is information."

I answered that I felt uncomfortable and that I didn't have the makings of a community leader. He assured me that I wouldn't have to fight anything but simply to inform them.

I came down full of blueprints and maps. They asked me what was going on. I showed them the tragedy that they themselves had provoked by selling their land. I told them, "You sold the lands of the Refuge—the lands of paradise—for a bowl of lentil stew. Now your paradise is valued in dollars, and nothing more will be left of it than a noisy, cemented seashore, like Cancún. But the pockets of many men will be overflowing. Six or seven men will have so much money that it is disgusting to name the exact figures."

They looked at each other.

"But is she trustworthy?"

"But what's Cancún?"

"But is the information in those blueprints true?"

"But what should we do?"

I tell them I don't have any answers. They say I must have answers since I work in the Ministry. I repeat that all I do in the Ministry is to try to get the Vice-Minister to stop the destruction.

One of the men gets up; he is not black. He exhorts the blacks to defend what is theirs—at least what little remains.

"Block the highways, burn tires; I want to see the blacks get angry," he tells them. "Make the central government know that you love this place and want to protect it."

"How should we protect it? What does 'protect' mean? What is ours? Who are we? What is the value of the Refuge?" they all interject at once.

"Believe me: the value of the Refuge is now incalculable," I tell them. "Unique plants, complex ecosystems. The cure for AIDS could come from these forest plants! If the Refuge is developed, you will lose all that."

"What should we do? What should we do?" they repeat anxiously.

"The only thing I can recommend is that you demand a modest, small-scale, truly ecological kind of tourism that won't harm the natural surroundings. And demand direct participation in the development as full partners and not merely as waiters and servants."

I don't know if they understand me.

They take with them the scientific document on the Refuge's extraordinary biodiversity. They schedule another meeting with me in two weeks.

"I'm at your service," I tell them.

Two weeks later I'm back. The meeting is big. They've come by land and sea.

They've come from remote farms up in the mountains and out along the sea. They know nothing—how could they know? To look for a neighbor takes them days, to find a telephone takes them weeks. It's also difficult to get papers, for here the print becomes illegible with the torrential rains: even if they put the papers under their clothes, it does no good, for everything gets drenched. Whether out of suspicion, curiosity, or good faith, they have come in the sweltering midday heat with their clothes all wet and muddy, walking over trails and shortcuts made by eager woodcutters.

Robinson had explained to me a long time ago that the communities had not wanted the Wildlife Refuge to be established. They feared that their land would be expropriated without payment, as had actually occurred to blacks living in the Cahuita National Park. But they got used to living with the Refuge, and some have even come to see that a Wildlife Refuge is for their own good.

Nevertheless, due to fear of the Refuge, many of them sold their lands dirt cheap. But they keep living there with less land and sometimes with only a hut, as if dispossessed.

Here I am watching them and aware of that. They are poor in one of the richest lands in the world.

I suddenly feel a strong urge to drop the whole affair and run away.

They begin the meeting. The ones who came to the first meetings explain things to the new ones. They decide to organize. Exactly at that moment a shiver of hope runs through me. I tell them that if they unite and agree on what to do, they'll be able to stop the destruction of the forest and the paving of the seashore. I advise them to manage the development themselves, like the indians in San Blas do.

It was after that meeting that a man with an artificial voice called me. He was a businessman—not a very respected one—who had had ten coronary bypasses. A short while ago he had acquired a large farm in the Refuge for a song. His farm was in Punta Uva.

First he tried to buy me off. Since he couldn't, he accused me of being a communist; then he called me a liar, saying, "You're fooling the blacks; this area isn't a Refuge."

He didn't let me answer. He assured me that no one had any intention of urbanizing or developing the Refuge because it was pure marshes. Then he warned me that if I kept meeting with the communities, I'd be in big trouble. That was all.

Then I realized why his voice was artificial and his skin plastic. My words slipped and would keep slipping off his skin because community control and regulation of tourism would place his business interests in jeopardy. I realized that the man with the ten bypasses was one of those who would become a millionaire by speculating on land in the Refuge. His intention was to urbanize the Refuge, and he told me that at last without any elegance: "Whether you are opposed or not, the Refuge is going to be built up; get that through your head." And he hung up.

The call was a declaration of war, but I didn't realize that until later on.

Your third detoxification is going full steam ahead, but you don't go anywhere without me. When I'm not around, the liquor is too dangerously enticing. My name is no longer Daniela—it's seatbelt.

After two months you try to be by yourself a bit. You tell me, "Tonight, I'm going out with some friends, and while they drink, I'll just have a Coke." I don't say anything; I just look at you. You insist, "I'm going out tonight without you, and I'm not going to drink. This will be my baptism, my test of fire."

I know that you won't pass the test of fire because your new friends are superficial and alcoholic, and the only thing that ties you to them is your addiction. What are you going to talk about with them if you remain sober?

Throughout the afternoon, you call me several times to repeat, "Today is my test of fire."

At quarter past six, you call me again in a tremulous voice: "The fiesta is for Javier's wife. They want you to come."

I feel like a manipulated mother; I am aware of your desperation. If I refuse to accompany you, you will plunge into the abyss. If I agree to accompany you, I will just be contributing to your self-deception. I see your beautiful masculine hands, so fine and sensual, clutching my skirt desperately. I don't know what to do.

You came home at six-thirty. You kissed the children, made sure that they were calmly eating with the maid, and you took me to our bedroom. You shut the door.

"Daniela," you said. "Daniela, Daniela." There was so much love and emotion in your voice that I returned to that world that you had given me: the sea and the children, the light and the shadow, the happiness. Love, or the memory of it, shut my throat. I knew beyond all words how dreadful and unjust it was to lose you.

You opened the buttons of my blouse very slowly. Slowly, very slowly, you kissed my nipples. You took my clothes off, and the tremulous anxiety in your fingers revealed how deep and overwhelming was the attraction we still felt. We came together in the exact sense of the biblical commandment: we were one flesh. I reflected that for every woman, there was a man, just one, destined to be one flesh with her. So in my whole life, I was only going to experience this more-than-bodily union with you. I had never experienced it before with any other man, and I wouldn't experience it ever again. I decided to stay with you.

You didn't mention the tests of fire again until you announced one day, "Danny, this detoxification has been a success. I've already been on the wagon for three months, and here I am safe and sane without valium and without being interned in a hospital. You see, love, I told you—I'm no longer alcoholic. I'm going to start drinking like most people do: just a little bit. I repeat, Daniela, that I'm no longer alcoholic. Believe me. Is there any way an alcoholic could stop drinking for so many months with so little trouble?"

I was thinking that there are alcoholics who stopped drinking for twenty, thirty years and kept being alcoholics. But I didn't tell you. What would be the use?

The seashore terrifies me. I don't want to go to Punta Uva.

You start to get ready for the vacation. Your urgency in going to the beach strikes me as suspicious. What do you want to prove to yourself?

"Nothing, I don't want to prove anything. There's a four-day weekend coming up, four wonderful days to rest," you explain in a suave voice.

"Let's rest here," I propose.

'Let's rest there," you insist, "at the most beautiful site in the world. We're not going to let our beach-house go to waste, are we?" I tell you firmly that I don't want to go. "Why, why?" you ask desolately. "Please, Daniela, come on, let's go—the whole family."

I don't want to go to that house because the glassy-green sea terrifies me—a visceral terror that I can't explain to you.

You spend hours trying to convince me, but I'm not going along with you. I can't.

It's the first time that I leave you alone during the detoxification.

You're getting in the car with a suitcase. The children ask, "Why is he going by himself?" I remind them that they have exams and that I have too much work—which is, by the way, quite true—and that's why we can't go. We say adios from the front door of the house. It's Friday.

"I'll be back Monday afternoon," you shout from the car.

I wake up happy. The children behave like angels and study while I work. Later we go to the pool. At the pool, I decide to take you at your word. I'm going to believe you, believe that you're not an alcoholic or at least that you're going to be cured and that we will once again be a normal and happy family without that murderous demon that forms in your eyes, without that thirst that tears you away from my side at night. I try to remember magazines I have seen with titles such as "I Was an Alcoholic" or "My Problem and How I Overcame It." I give myself up shamelessly to hope; I let myself feast on it. The children ask, "Why are you so happy?"

When I return home after swimming, your sister is waiting for me with dark glasses. Behind the sunglasses, her eyes are red. She hugs me and asks the maid to take the children to the playroom.

"What's wrong, Virginia?"

"Daniela, last night Carlos Manuel had an accident."

"An accident? What happened? Is it serious?"

Virginia nods her head yes, crying. She can't speak. The telephone rings. It's my father-in-law. He too has just been informed that his son had a serious accident and that they are already bringing him back to San José.

"But Virginia, tell me, is he in a coma? What kind of accident was it?"

"It seems that he went to a party at Stanford's in Puerto Viejo on Friday night. He drank a lot, took off like a bullet for home, and went off a bridge. The car fell into the river."

"What happened to him? Is it serious?"

Virginia pauses.

"Did he drown?"

She confirms, "Yes, Daniela, Carlos Manuel is dead."

Many months after his death, I start to emerge from a cold and black well. First I put my fingers up. I place them between the stones, hold tight, and push. Then I pull my arms out. What a delight to feel the sun on my arms.

I could have stayed for months hanging by my arms and hiding the rest of myself while coming very slowly out of the well. I would have remained hanging and hidden for many months if it hadn't been for Dominique. Some piercing shrieks punctured my eardrum; it was her voice on Punta Uva. Trembling, I leaped abruptly out of my lethargy and stood up.

"Hey, what are you making?" I asked her.

"Some cabins," she said in French.

"Oh, you're the French woman."

"Sixteen cabins, my house, a restaurant, and a dance club."

"Here, just ten meters from my house?"

"Yes."

"You can't just build like that," I said stretching out, trying to accustom myself to warmth, to life, trying to remember where I was—oh, yes, "You can't just build like that because this is a Wildlife Refuge."

"I have all of the permits."

"Wait, do you have the Ministry of Health permit?

"No!"

"The permit from the Institute of Tourism?"

"No!"

"The permit from the Director of the Refuge, the one from Wildlife?"

"No, not that one either, but I have the municipal permit."

"It's no good—it's not enough."

Dominique resumed her shrieks, probably so as to make me leave. Confused, I stretched my body, which was the color of an egg white for having been submerged so many months in the well. I was thinking that she wouldn't dare to build without the various ministry permits.

I left the French woman with the sharp tongue and the rapacious face behind.

I went into the kitchen. The children were eating with the maid. All three shouted, "Mommy, Mommy, you're resurrected!"

"If you only knew how unpleasant my resurrection has been!"

"What really matters is that you want to live again," said the eldest.

I was thinking that I wasn't too sure of that, but perhaps it would come about by the sheer struggle of trying to keep up appearances in front of them.

I walked to the site of the accident, and I recalled the police report: "We found the dead body in the water at the mouth of the river."

I went there to cry. It was the same river and beach where you had made love to me the first time.

"Yemanyá, Yemanyá," I shouted desperately, "That warm and eager body that I had loved more than my own is now dead. You took it away from me."

"It wasn't me," the Goddess immediately replied. "It was the river. The rivers belong to Oxum. Go complain to her."

I went to Oxum with my grievance. I had been looking at the river so sadly that I had not seen the cans in the bottom, the plastic bottles that floated by, and a gathering yellowish scum. All the trees had been cut down on the bank, and the mud was being washed away. The sewage from various cabins also emptied into the river. It turned my stomach.

Then my sadness turned to rage, I stopped thinking about Carlos Manuel's death, and instead of complaining to Oxum, I decided to complain to the Wildlife Office.

I called Wildlife countless times. Either no one answered, or I got the busy signal. Then I went in person to the Ministry of Natural Resources.

Ana Luisa stopped calling me. Since her silence was painful to me, I called her.

"I'm very busy, Daniela. What can I help you with?"

"Has the Vice-Minister read the Institute for the Study of Flora's report on the extraordinary biodiversity of the Refuge?"

"I don't know."

"Am I still in charge of the Gandoca Refuge Defense Project?"

"Yes, but I have already told you that the Minister wants you to leave. He says that you don't have the right character to be an official—that you're too aggressive. Everyone in the Ministry agrees that you're too aggressive."

"And what do you think?"

"That you're a woman with rough edges. Why don't you get yourself a massage?"

You're so nice, my friend. What would I do without you in this plain and barren desert that is widowhood? You accompany the children and me to Punta Uva.

I show you the treasured beauty of the marine night. When the children fall asleep, we stay up talking in the corridor. We speak softly, like people in church, out of respect for the inner depth of the night.

"I hate myself for not having controlled myself at the last meeting of the ministry," I say in a whisper.

"Don't torture yourself."

"Ana Luisa's right; I was too aggressive."

"That's just the pretext they were seeking to marginalize you."

"If I had behaved properly, they couldn't marginalize me now."

"Yes, they could. They would just find another pretext."

"But why?"

"Daniela, you're as naïve as you are pretty. You denounced the Minister's game plan to the Attorney General."

"It was my duty."

"Anyone who does her duty in the Ministry is dangerous. They won't rest until they've gotten rid of you."

"Ana Luisa will defend me."

"She's not going to risk her job for you. Is it true that there's a meeting tomorrow?"

Yes, there is a meeting in the fishermen's village. I'm getting in my car when a neighbor arrives to tell me that the bridge has been deliberately weakened.

"Who weakened it?"

Silence.

This stinks to me of the man with the ten bypasses.

"Okay, we'll go on foot."

But the people of the communities are organized: they take us to the bridge in a four-wheel drive vehicle, we cross it on foot, and a vehicle picks us up on the other side.

It's the biggest turnout we've had yet, but it has already been undermined, like worm-filled fruit. The man with the ten bypasses and other contractors have been at work planting seeds of distrust and discord. Mutual suspicions erupt. People attack each other. Dozens of countrypeople who have come hopefully from far away are suddenly fighting and pulling each other's hair.

The shallow, greenish-blue reef waters lie before us. A snorkeler appears a long way out with water up to his knees. I think that the beauty of the scene is tormenting, piercing, because, as a Nahuatl poem states, "a wind as sharp as obsidian is blowing upon us now." How many years of this paradise are left? One? Two?

"How did it go?" you ask when I return, my friend. The children surround me.

"Hey, who are those people over there?"

"Dominique's workers. They've already begun construction. They're digging thousands of ditches."

Exhausted as I am from the worm-filled meeting, I rush to the end of my patio and ask the workers to stop digging that ditch, because at high tide the sea could come in and carry my house away. The workers stop what they're doing and leave.

A half hour later, a policeman from Puerto Viejo arrives with Dominique. The policeman says that if I try to stop the workers from finishing their ditch, which isn't on my property but on public land, he will take me to jail. Dominique smiles with evident satisfaction.

When they leave, you say, "Don't be surprised. A while ago we went to the *pulpería*, and some people there were saying that Dominique claims she paid several million colones to obtain the municipal building permit. Now, who knows how much she paid the policeman?"

"Look, I bet she probably didn't have to give him anything."

There was a long rainy spell after that meeting; two bridges fell down, and we were cut off from Talamanca. For a time, I didn't know if the only resolution agreed to at the worm-infested meeting had been fulfilled, which was that every community in the Refuge should let the government know what it thought concerning development, conservation, and tourism.

One of the community leaders telephoned me; he wanted to tell me that his community had organized and that the country people were going to ask the government to work with the community to design development projects that would leave the forests intact and that meanwhile the government should provide them with food and supplies for subsistence so that hunger wouldn't force them to cut down the trees.

I thought it was a great idea.

It was the morning of my middle child's First Communion.

"Mommy, Ana Luisa is on the phone."

I heard the strong, hoarse, peremptory voice of the woman for whom I had felt such affection.

"How are you, Daniela?"

"Fine but in a rush; today is my son's First Communion. In less than half an hour we're going to church, and I'm still dressing him."

"I want to tell you something that I hope you won't take the wrong way. Daniela, the people from the Refuge are saying HORRIBLE things about you, just HORRIBLE things."

"What are they saying?"

"That you're meddling in the affairs of the community, that you're a drunk and a drug addict, that all of the Rastafarians are your lovers, and that you get so plastered you drop in the bars of Puerto Viejo."

"Why are you telling me this, Ana Luisa? Who told you?"

"I can't tell you; I heard it through the grapevine. But I advise you not to have any more than one drink in public."

"I never drink . . ."

"Everyone hates you."

"This must be the work of the man with the ten bypasses."

"They're saying horrible things about you, horrible things. Oh, I also have something else to tell you, Daniela. The Minister has fired you. And he has authorized the 'Ecodollars' project."

"What about the technical reports that the Vice-Minister received? Doesn't he care if they urbanize the Refuge?"

"The Vice-Minister tried to oppose the project, but he couldn't. The Constitutional Tribunal has ordered that private property cannot be regulated."

"And why don't they expropriate it?"

"Because there's no money to expropriate it."

"And what are the Attorney for the Environment and the biologists saying? Isn't this driving them nuts?"

"What the Attorney for the Environment or the biologists say isn't of the least importance in this case."

None of the community leaders called me again. None of the communities communicated anything to the government. None even made a single proclamation. No more meetings were convened.

When I got back to Punta Uva, not a single member of the community came up the stairs of my cottage looking for me. Silence reigned, broken only by the rumble of the heavy machinery in several tourist developments, including Dominique's.

What Dominique was building just ten meters from my house was a small-scale housing development. She didn't have a single required permit. She had already built eight cabins, the restaurant, the dance club, her house, and the parking lot. The project had no sanitary system: the septic tanks of the cabins were small sewers of less than one square meter, and the sewage emptied through plastic pipes directly into ditches and then into the sea. The septic tanks were so close to the sea and to my own fresh-water well that it didn't take a genius to realize that contamination was inevitable.

I had gone from one government office to another, denouncing the illegality and the lack of controls. I wrote to the Forestry Office, which was in charge of the Refuge. They laughed their heads off at my letters. I also wrote to the Vice-Minister, since Dominique's tourist development was not on private property but rather on the public shoreline area, and thus she was not protected by any supposed decree of the Constitutional Tribunal. In reply, the Vice-Minister had raised his arms to the sky and, bending his nose even further out of joint, shouted, "I don't want to know anything about French women!" Other ministries issued orders to stop her, but the orders had apparently dissipated on the way, for the construction continued full steam ahead. They were already roofing the cabins.

I sought out Dominique and told her, "You need to install a sewage treatment plant. This land is clayey, coralline, rainy, and marshy, besides being such a small plot. The excrement from your tourists is going to wash into my well and onto the beach. My children could become ill. You must put in a sewage treatment plant."

"By no means—treatment plants are way too expensive. The government of this country should send a truck to pick up the shit from my septic tanks. That's what they do on the Côte d'Azur of France."

Dominique had vast wealth. She said that her family had made the money building dance clubs and restaurants in Nice, and now she was utterly determined to do the same in the Gandoca Refuge.

"We don't want you to open a dance club, because we like to hear the sea and the birds, Dominique. We have a right to peace and quiet."

"I built them in Nice, a civilized place, and you're going to tell me that I can't build them here!" she shouted furiously.

I went to look for the community leader who had told me about asking the government for subsistence food and supplies. He was dry and distant. His enthusiasm had vanished as if swallowed by the earth.

"Look, Daniela, they say that you're opposed to progress and prosperity. I think that progress is necessary here. The Italians' project is going to bring us work, money, advances. We shouldn't obstruct foreign investment."

"Name just one benefit that urbanization is going to bring the community."

"Employment, for example."

"Making beds and serving drinks."

"Any kind of work is good. Besides, the land will go up in value, and I have a piece of property I want to sell."

"Alright, see you later."

The men in the community would not greet me. When they saw me walking along the beach, even Wallis Black turned his head away.

Trudging slowly under the ponderous weight of my loneliness, I arrived at the Italians' property. I entered and felt its disquieting beauty. The tall trees blocked out the sky, and they were buttressed by massive wall-like roots. The dense jungle was teeming with ancient and useful species. The tangled jungle extended to a grove of coconut palms, and beyond them lay the white sand. The transition from jungle to beach was pristine and as yet untouched: the trees thinned out, and big, bright, endemic flowers such as *Heliconias* emerged, along with fruits such as the sea soursops and monkey fruits. The palm trees had orange trunks, and they were overrun with orchids in full bloom. All of this was soon going to disappear beneath the bulldozers, excavators, and Caterpillar tractors.

A land turtle came out of the marsh. I stopped to watch it. Its shell was covered with leeches. I could imagine the Italians spraying poison for the tortoises because—horrors, horrors—there were leeches.

All this was going to disappear in order to build beauty salons, dance clubs, stores, restaurants, tennis courts, pools, bungalows, level streets, and clean lots without puddles, without those bothersome plants that the crabs eat, and, above all, without trees. The Italians' "Ecodollars" Company wanted to sell so many lots that every lot had to be small, and even one single tree would impede construction.

We used to come here together, Carlos Manuel. You liked to wander around the buggy marsh and then lie down in the pale sand. You would hug me, kiss me, and beg me to sing you that Creole song from Martinique. The words sunk into the underbrush, into the waves, into your beautiful yellow-green eyes. *Lan mé' a ka gémi, la lun'lan ka frémi, cocotiers kapa'lé, caressé moin, caressé moin* ("The sea moans, the moon shivers, the coconut palms murmer, caress me, caress me") *Solei la ka plewé, la lun'lan ka chiwé, cocotiers ka flambé, caressé moin, caressé moin* ("The sun is crying, the moon has withdrawn, the coconut palms are burning, caress me, caress me").

The sun is crying, and you're no longer here to console it. The coconut palms will burn like trash. The moon has withdrawn, and you're no longer here to caress me.

The sun doesn't sink into the sea; it sinks behind the mountain, behind the line of cawi trees, *cativos*, and *guácimos*. The trees will die, and you're already dead. Caress me, caress me, Carlos Manuel.

Drying my tears, I entered the café, ordered a soft drink, and sat in a corner.

Concealed behind a plant's abundant foliage, I saw them arrive. The plant's large fronds were like a curtain, and the three men sat down near me without knowing it. They were the Minister, the man with the ten bypasses, and a congressman whom I recognized immediately: he had appeared in all of the papers, accused of having drafted laws in his own self-interest. The Minister was laughing incessantly; he ordered a beer and arranged the flowery hem of his matching Bermuda shorts and shirt. The man with the ten bypasses was wearing a leather jacket in spite of the suffocating heat, and he pulled out a bottle of whiskey.

The Minister looked around him to make sure that the three of them were alone, and then he uttered, "They say that that madwoman Daniela Zermat hangs out around here."

My stomach turned.

"Don't worry; she's been neutralized," replied the man with the ten bypasses. We've already convinced all of the blacks that she can't be trusted and that all she wants is for the communities to starve to death."

"Did you also tell them that the hotels will bring them a lot of money?" asked the Minister.

"Of course."

"Remember, we have to tell them that every hotel room will generate at least one job directly and a couple more on the side. Don't tell them anything about the housing development," advised the Minister.

"My project is all ready. As soon as definitive permission is granted to 'Ecodollars,' I'll launch it. I guarantee you that this place is a gold mine—all of the people with money are going to want to buy property here; the beach is beautiful. I guarantee that this investment is 100% safe. Do you know for sure when the definitive approval will be given to 'Ecodollars'? The Italians are really eager to get started, and so am I."

"A minor detail was lacking to complete the bureaucratic requirements of the Refuge's Regulations: the Italians hadn't presented an environmental impact study. That other madwoman, Ana Luisa, threatened to blow the whistle if I gave them definitive approval without that study. The Italians have assured me that it's almost ready. At precisely the hour they hand in the document, I will give them full permission, and the next day the bulldozers will go in and flatten the jungle."

"Daniela keeps trying to blow the whistle on the housing development, and that worries me," said the congressman.

"I'm sure there won't be any problems with the housing development, because it will be done on private property. I told the Italians not even to include it in the impact study because we're going to use the Constitutional Tribunal decree in our favor. If there were any problems—which I doubt—the project will be proposed without the housing development, and we'll just add it in later. Once the machinery has leveled the jungle, no one will be able to stop the housing development—I'm the Minister, and I say so!"

Raucous laughter.

"If the madwoman still has you worried," the man with the ten bypasses said softly, "don't worry: I'm starting a movement in the community to have her declared *non grata* and have her run out of here. I already have the members of the Development Association convinced. Setting the community against her in particular and against conservation in general will get the best results. The slogan could be, 'Conservation means starvation."

"Perfect. Don't forget the magic word: 'sustainable development.' We have to present the 'Ecodollars' project as sustainable development," added the Minister. And, I repeat, never mention the housing development."

"How fortunate it is, besides, that the madwoman has problems with the Frenchwoman who is building those awful cabins and the dance club just behind her house," said the artificial man.

"The Frenchwoman is carrying out that development thanks to me," said the Minister. "I stopped the inspection that Daniela requested when her neighbor started to build. Fortunately, the Vice-Minister can't stand Daniela. Otherwise, they would have stopped that housing development a long time ago—she's building without a single permit."

"Son of a bitch, that French woman is brave; I take my hat off to her," added the man with the ten bypasses. "Daring to build without a single permit!"

"For your information, there are two other developments without permits," clarified the Minister. "The world belongs to the people with guts."

"Let me tell you guys about the new farm I bought—fifty acres," said the artificial man.

"No, not now," exclaimed the congressman. "The girls are coming."

I took advantage of the wives' or mistresses' arrival and left, screening myself with the fronds of the plant.

How can I not yearn for you, Carlos Manuel? But yearning for you isn't enough.

I stretch out my hands and let my hair cover me so that the Goddess can measure, inch by inch, how long it has grown. It covers my face and almost my entire body. No one sees me. It is a savage rite performed only in solitude.

I begin by invoking the starfish wrapped around my wrists many years ago. I continue with the octopuses, the ones I have hunted for food and those that I have pursued for observation. I move on to the anemones, to the sponges, to the coral whose tortuous design is like that of the convolutions of a brain, then to the coral which is like extended tables, or like big round armchairs. I follow up with the infinite variety of multicolored organisms that flutter and undulate, mother of the sea, my only mistress. Your long green hair is warm and slimy—it is woven by the sea with threads of turtle grass.

I have loved your kingdom as one loves a man. I know your territory like the back of my hand. I hear you roar in the stormy afternoons. On those dark afternoons, the trade winds push the sky aside to make way for themselves; they tear the leaves off the coconut palms, and the rainstorm beats us in heavy gusts. It is your vitality that beats like a big drum.

Together we have cried from happiness; together we have eaten decaying seaweed; together we have made up songs about seashells and sung them to the children when they can't fall asleep. Together we have washed the beach's gold; together we have sworn to be faithful to the sickening and obscene aroma of your lairs. Don't forsake me now.

Don't abandon me to the onslaught of the European destroyer and of the fickle black. Come, listen to me; I'm kneeling on a formation of old coral, and my knees bear the imprint of the pores. I'm kneeling, almost prostrate; I'm bent forward like a Muslim during prayer, with my forehead in the water. I glimpse your long crown of ghosts, Goddess of the drowned, Mother of the sea.

Yemanyá, Señora, I am desperate. Grant me advice or protection.

"Let's be more concrete—we have to be practical," roars the Goddess.

"I've tried all of the administrative ploys, and I haven't been able to defend either myself or the plant life. Your entire beach is becoming polluted, and the forest is dying. No one cares. They just want to get rid of me. What should I do?"

"The situation looks grim," says the Goddess of foam. "Let me think."

An underwater whirlpool forms, a tip of the crown of ghosts emerges, and she affirms, "You feel forsaken. Ask the Constitutional Tribunal for help."

"No, Goddess, I just heard the Minister, who was rubbing his hands together, mention that the Constitutional Tribunal upholds destruction."

"I'm not so sure of that," says the Goddess. "But if it is true, ask the Constitutional Tribunal to say so publicly and indicate who should shoulder the costs of the destruction. In any event, you can ask nobody else for help—no one, Daniela, not your mother, not your father, not your dead husband, not even me."

Mariana doesn't understand my urgency in appealing to the Constitutional Tribunal for help. But she's quite bright and prolific, and she has accumulated so many notes and so much evidence of misconduct, absence, negligence, and foolishness of the institution governing our natural resources that it turns out to be easy for her to draft a brilliant legal case.

In effect, Mariana shows that the Ministry is violating Articles 6, 23, 24, 45, 50, and 89 of the Political Constitution of our country; Article 18 of the Wildlife Law; Article 1 of the Refuge Creation Act; Articles 3, 4, 9, and 10 of the Refuge Regulation Act; the Forestry Law; the Central American Convention on Environment and Development; The Convention for the Protection of the Flora, of the Fauna, and of the Scenic Natural Beauties of the Countries of America; The Convention for the Protection of Natural and Cultural Heritage; The Convention Relating to Marshes of International Importance Especially As Habitat of Aquatic Birds; and The Convention for the Protection and Development of the Marine Environment of the Greater Caribbean Region. The Appeal is a thirty-page document, and Mariana appends four hundred more pages of pictures and evidence. She asks me to write an anecdotal brief so that the Judges can situate themselves in the case.

Here, from the Executive Act that created the Gandoca Refuge based on the Wildlife Law and the Forestry Law, from the dark and wonderful swamp, from the unique and extraordinary association of the different varieties of Raphia palms, from the last source of mangrove oyster (*Crassostrea rhizophorea*), and from this warm little hole of sand, I ask you to help me, Honorable Justices of the Constitutional Tribunal. Save me from life gone astray. Trees fall in the rumble of chainsaws; pools and streams dry up; and my eyes have also dried, Honorable Justices. Save me from the authority of the state that accuses me of every crime

74

when in reality I have only committed a sin: that of asking that the laws be applied. Honorable Justices, help me and issue a well-founded verdict: define once and for all whether it is a sin, a crime, an offense, or a virtue to defend beauty. I confess that I have a long-standing affinity with plant life. My arteries seem like roots, and I'm convinced that the flower of the blue mahoe is my skin. The skin of my hands gets wrinkled like the rough surface of the sea grape tree leaves with their protruding veins, a floral passion. And when I attend to the children, my hands have the leafy, encompassing spread and bitter sweetness of big almond trees.

Save me from those who, although designated by the will of the people to watch over the natural wealth of our nation, exploit their office for their own ends. Save me from the Minister who, with a smile on his face and a whiskey in his hand, illegally turns the coastal forests over to investors. Save me from the Minister, who, when I went to request a reasonable and foresighted management plan, threw me out into the street and fired me from the merely honorary position (no one paid me a cent) given to me by Ana Luisa and the Vice-Minister in the Ministry. The Vice-Minister's advisors moved their sage heads in consternation and murmured, "Poor, poor Daniela; they got rid of her because she is too passionate, too romantic." And I ask you, Honorable Justices, what is romantic about demanding that the law be applied?

In addition, I told the Minister that it would be irresponsible of him to cut the wetland forest of the Caribbean land to build an ice-skating rink. And the Minister answered, "Don't get mixed up in this, my dear little lady; don't impede progress. The blacks of this region are so poor and so backward that we're going to give them an opportunity to train to become champion ice-skaters and win all of the gold medals in the Winter Olympics. That way they'll overcome their lack of development. Besides, we're going to do it because it's a totally ecological ice-skating rink." But how are they going to offer ice-skating in such a hot and humid land! The Minister declared, "Yes, my dear lady, we have calculated the value of the steam vapor that rises from the nearby forest, the exact amounts of evapotranspiration and of condensation, etc. This whole tropical natural process is a source of fabulous energy that will move steam turbines to cool the water and transform it into ice. As you see, it's a totally ecological process, my dear lady." The scientific part sounds okay to me, I answered, but you are counting on the steam and the vapor that rise from the forest, and the investors WILL LEVEL THE FOREST. The Minister shrugged, adding, "We have to let them cut down the forest, my dear lady; there is no other remedy. But inside the Refuge and far from the coast, there is a farm that won't be cut down, because the organization called Green World bought it for conservation. We'll bring the vapor and the energy from that farm. The rest of the Refuge will have to be destroyed if the owners want to, because it's private property. The Constitutional Tribunal has so decreed."

Is that true, Honorable Justices?

Save me also from the Vice-Minister, who is indirectly delegated by the people to protect their natural resources from depredation and from arbitrary interests. Save me from this famous conservationist, Honorable Justices, because every time I ask him to stop the cutting of trees and building of hotels and cabins without permits, he plays deaf. Every time I tell him that Dominique has, without even a permit, opened a deep wound in the Gandoca Refuge, through which suds and sewage will flow like the tears of misfortune and make my children ill; every time I inform him that Dominique will leave us without water, silence, or wildlife and will open a gambling joint with drugs and alcohol behind the tree where the large anteaters and little raccoons live; every time I ask him to use the power invested in him by the people to protect me, to protect all of us from the disturbance and from the pollution that will go straight into the sea, the Vice-Minister raises his hands toward heaven, bends his nose out of joint, and furiously exclaims, "I don't want to hear anything more about Frenchwomen!"

Save me, too, invincible Justices, from the lawyers and other officials of the Forestry Office who laugh delightedly at my discomfort, and who rub their hands together in glee every time a tree falls: "One less to protect" they say; "Oh, what a relief; let them all fall—it wears us out just to think of defending them. Let the country go to ruin."

Save me very particularly from the officials of the Forestry Office of Limón, whom I called many months ago to announce that trees were being cut on the banks of the rivers of the Gandoca Refuge in the last remaining forests to the south of that province. They answered, "That's not under our jurisdiction, Señora."

"The trees on the banks of the rivers of Limón are under the jurisdiction of the Forestry Office of Limón."

"That's strange."

"Right here in front of my eyes is a copy of the law, along with another document that says that the national wildlife refuges are under the jurisdiction of the Forestry Office."

"That's even stranger. . . . Where did you say that cutting is going on?"

"In the Gandoca Refuge, to the south of Limón."

"Oh, the Gandoca Refuge is so far away. If we go, we'll get lost."

"You can't get lost; it's just a matter of taking the highway and going straight. All these rivers cross the highway. The cutting is going on in sight of the road."

"Oh no. You see, every time we go south, we get lost."

Here from my warm little hole in the sand, hidden from the eyes of the great blue herons, the pelicans, and the kingfisher, surrounded by sea grape trees whose green and bittersweet clusters of grapes hang close above the water; here from my warm little hole in the sand next to the slimy pastures of turtle grass, in the breakers formed by the outer and inner coral reefs, buoyed up by the waves, desperate, sick of waiting, from among the blue mahoes and the coco plums and the *Heliconias* and the wild lilies, intoxicated by odors that are going to disappear forever, full of sun and of rain, I ask you to help us, Honorable Justices.

The high officials entrusted with watching over our natural wealth are destroying it or exchanging it for dollars, and they say it is by your mandate.

Please clarify your position for me, oh Highest Power in the land.

My children are worried: "Mommy, Mommy, don't let the destruction get you down so much." I gaze at you firmly, my friend. My children have called you because they are anxious at seeing me run all around. You have come tonight to give me advice. You also tell me not to worry so much about a problem that is general and worldwide. You say that progress is a bulldozer, a steamroller; that all of the European consortia have their eyes fixed on our fragile coasts because, like pimps, our leaders traveled to the four corners of the developed world to sell our beaches, wiggling their own rear ends temptingly in the process; and that our country is no longer ours.

No, this region no longer belongs to us. First, it ceased to belong to the indians, then it ceased to belong to the blacks, and later it ceased to belong to the Costa Ricans in general. I saw that in the eyes of the policeman from Puerto Viejo when he came to handcuff me and throw me in prison for opposing the destruction caused by a Frenchwoman who had not even lived here one year. "Don't obstruct foreign investment, Señora; move along, now, move along."

In the dollar-, progress-, and commotion-filled eyes of the millionaire Dominique, I saw that we had lost the coast and its beauty. I was small, fragile, and native. Too romantic, as Ana Luisa claimed. I realized that when I read the record of Luigi Calzoni, the president of "Ecodollars," Inc., with its massive hotels in Italy, Brazil, Barbados, the Dominican Republic, etc.

My children are worried and anxious. And as always when I don't know what to say to them, when I am ashamed of my failures or of my useless efforts— when I was struggling against their father's alcoholism, for example—as always when I am full of doubts, I propose that we climb the mountain.

I come here to think. In these cold mountains, the clarity is penetrating. At my feet, below, far down below, lies the capital bordered by the hills to the south. And behind those hills, others. The view is so great that various mountain ranges can be seen. The cypress trees, bent by the northeast wind, descend in an orderly army almost to the city.

Night has fallen on the mountain. I told the children, "I'm going to the lake. I'll be back soon. Don't any of you even think of hunting or grabbing the common pauraques. They're magical birds."

I ascended to the lake along the path of cypress and cedar trees in the cold and moonlit night. The wind in the trees sounded like the sea, damn it! I cradled and lulled myself, and I cried; I cried remembering.

I was lying down and given over to my pain and sobbing when a fat green disheveled bug arrived. I recognized it in an instant: it was the "lord of the thicket," a legendary entity of Costa Rican fables and fairy tales, somewhat like the green man of Europe.

"The first thing I'm going to ask you, Daniela, is to clarify for your readers that I am neither a metaphor nor a stylistic device, nor is this an instance of magical realism. My presence is authentic."

"Your clarification won't work. I just explained to my children that the common pauraque is a magical bird. Therefore, you could also occupy that category."

"Yes, I am magical, but not because your style demands it, if you know what I mean. Explain that I am a spirit of the forests, the spirit of the wilderness. Explain that you have botanical allies, natural allies."

"Natural allies?—the river swallowed my husband."

"It swallowed him just in time, before he destroyed all of your love. Besides, we let you know."

"What did you let me know?"

"That death was stalking him and that you shouldn't go. We warned you three times."

"Is that so?"

"Of course. Don't you remember? The first time was the cry of a bird."

"I remember that heart-rending bird."

"The second was by means of the trees, which also happened at night."

When he said this, I suddenly remembered the scene as if I were reliving it, as if I had been transported back to that very night. We were in our house on Punta Uva, and I couldn't sleep. Whenever I suffer from insomnia, I think of peaceful things to lull myself. That night I thought about the trees on the patio, the ones closest to the beach. I was starting to fall asleep picturing them when, all of a sudden, I clearly sensed that I was part of them. I saw myself outside, high up, watching the birds, moving my leaves. It was a delightful sensation to be part of a tree, part of the birds and of the warm night. My arms, legs, and hair were floating. It was a wonderful sensation, as if I had been freed of everything. The wind caressed me because I was a little leaf, a trunk, an owl, a swaying movement. A voice said in my ear that this is the way it would be when I died, that death would feel this way. I realized that the process was beginning and that dying was being part of the wind, of the trees, and of the animals. An overwhelming terror filled me and brought me back to my bed. I touched my arms and legs; I was alive and whole, but something within the trees was calling me to death, to the delight that it was to die—to die, to dissolve, to float on the wind. I awoke Carlos Manuel and told him, "Death is outside in the trees of the patio, and it is delightful. If I drop my guard, if I fall asleep, it will take me." Carlos Manuel didn't pay any attention to me; he merely turned over and kept snoring. I stayed awake until daybreak, and after that night I didn't go back to Punta Uva. It terrified me. I began to suffer from panic attacks.

"That was the third warning: the terror. For some reason you didn't accompany him that weekend. We made you fear the house and flee the sea."

"That's absolutely right."

"Well, what I want to tell you now is that you must prepare yourself."

"To suffer more?"

"Yes."

"But why?"

"Hasn't Mariana told you? The Ministry of Natural Wealth has turned out a document with its new political strategy: it's going to divide and nullify all of the parks, reserves, refuges, and protected areas that aren't indemnified. It's going to hand them over to companies specializing in mining, tourism, banana cultivation, dairy production, etc. We Lords of the Thicket have already sounded the alarm, and millions of species are packing their bags and picking up their nests, preparing themselves for emigration."

"They don't have anywhere to go."

"We're making a map of the lands that have been expropriated and paid off in the parks. We'll go there. Of course, there are other dangers: many parks are next to banana plantations, and we know that contact with agricultural chemicals can deform or kill us. Other parks are crossed by highways, and the noise is maddening. In Braulio Carrillo Park, the noise of the highway echoes so loudly from mountain to mountain that all of the animals are seeing psychiatrists."

"Mariana, did you know that all of the animals at the Braulio Carrillo Park are seeing psychiatrists?"

"Yes. Some are even committing suicide. I have just received a report by some biologists about that."

The report was terrible. She also noted that there were four hundred proposals for tourist projects in the park's buffer zone alone. And that the

Minister was seeking to reform the law in order to build facilities inside the parks in general and permit prospecting and mining, etc. Besides, all of the parks had problems with funding and problems with private property and pollution. Twenty tons of garbage were removed daily from the Manuel Antonio National Park alone, and that park received millions of cubic meters of sewage. "The foreigners arrive and go swimming, and everything looks beautiful to them," said Mariana, "and they don't realize that they're swimming in shit. That's not even to mention the problems with the Corcovado National Park, the Carara Reserve, Tortuguero, Cahuita, and the Absolute Reserve of Cabo Blanco. . . . There are parks and reserves that in a few years will disappear. Nothing will remain, because it's estimated that Costa Rica will also have exhausted its commercial forests. It will have to import wood, and that will cost the country $375 million annually, according to the figures of the World Institute of Resources."

Mariana was exhausted from sending letters to all of the conservation organizations, scientific bodies, and clueless countries that were giving us prizes for conserving our natural wealth. Mariana went on denouncing abuse after abuse, all the while saying that it did little good but not knowing what else she could do.

"Mariana, do we have any chance of winning the appeal?"

"Unfortunately, I have no idea. Were you aware, by the way, that everybody calls the man with the ten bypasses "Cold Tiger"?

I feel as sad as a caged animal.

That is the way they make one feel, the discouragement that they bring about. Mariana and I asked the Constitutional Tribunal, as a cautionary measure, to stop the logging of the Refuge's forests, to suspend the "Ecodollars" permit, and to halt the construction of tourist projects that lacked the legally required permits.

My children beg me not to lose hope but instead to cling to it as to the cry of the last bird.

I can't ask my mother or father for help. I can't ask Carlos Manuel, who is dead, for help. I have no idea if the Constitutional Tribunal will help me. I am, without a doubt, in a state of almost utter helplessness.

I feel crushed, impotent. Now I can do nothing but wait and watch, wide-eyed, as the splendor of paradise is extinguished in gory detail.

I will at least watch it and tell of it, so that it will be known that paradise once existed. The Ministry has fired me, the community has ostracized me, and commercial interests seem about to triumph over health, beauty, and life. Now all that I have left is what Antonio Machado once observed in a poem: "*Me queda la palabra*"—I still have words, the power of speech, the chance to be heard.

And as Beto, a black from Cahuita, said, "History is words."

Words become history when a written record is left somewhere.

Where should I leave a record of the melancholy song of that smallest of toucans, the Emerald toucanet?

Who has heard it?

Mariana and I again asked the Constitutional Tribunal—having taken up my appeal and in keeping with the law of constitutional jurisdiction—to halt illegal tourist development.

Sometime later on a Monday, I showed up in the office of the Constitutional Secretary to see if there was an answer.

The Court's answer read, "The Talamanca Municipality is ordered to halt all construction in the Gandoca Wildlife Refuge that lacks a permit from the Ministry of Natural Wealth."

So the Municipality had to halt Dominique's mini-housing development and two or three other illegal projects immediately.

I remembered the millions that Dominique mentioned having given them for the municipal permit.

"Has this order already been sent to the Municipality?" I asked the court employee.

"Of course, a long time ago."

"Was the Municipality informed by letter or by telegraph?"

"I don't know."

"Could you find out for me? Because I was in the area yesterday, and the Municipality hasn't stopped anything."

No, it hadn't stopped anything. On Sunday, Dominique had looked at me with a smile of triumph while she hung a sign announcing the imminent inauguration of her restaurant, bar, *discothèque*, and hotel cabins, with reggae music so loud that it promised to raise the dead from their tombs. But it didn't announce the most important thing—its dumping of raw sewage directly onto the beach.

The Court clerk searched and could find no indication that the Municipality had been informed.

"I'm going to look into this," he said. "Come back tomorrow."

I went everyday for a week to the Court, but no sign of the message appeared. So the judges' assistants made a copy of the order and advised me to take it myself by commission to the Municipality of Talamanca in Bribri.

I drove for hours in torrential rains, hours of a bright green like wet rubber.

My older children accompanied me. Neither of them spoke much throughout the trip. When we left the coastal highway to turn toward the deforested mountain that leads to the indigenous town of Bribri, Andreas asked, "Do you think they're going to stop the Frenchwoman's dance club? The opening night is in two weeks, Mommy."

"Look, Andreas, if they don't halt it, they'll be guilty of contempt of court in the Constitutional Tribunal."

It was devilishly hot in Bribri. We handed over the Court's order.

The Municipality refused to obey. So Mariana told the story to the editor of a newspaper. A reporter went to Punta Uva immediately, and in twenty-four hours an article appeared with pictures: "The Municipality of Talamanca refuses to obey Constitutional Tribunal order."

The aldermen called me. They were clear, direct, repetititve: "We hate you, we hate you, we hate you, Daniela."

"What is hateful about trying to protect health and beauty?"

Against their will, the aldermen halted Dominique's tourist development.

I thought that the Frenchwoman would run to request permission from the Minister. But she didn't.

One oppressively hot and humid day, Dominique met in Bribri with the aldermen. I was in town and saw them by chance. Dominique walked into the office with loud steps. In a sharp French accent, she ordered, "Get rid of Daniela anyway you can. I'll pay whatever has to be paid. Expropriate her—according to the property marker, half of her patio is on public land."

"There's nothing we'd like to do more," answered a Municipality employee. "We can't stand her either, but expropriating her would mean expropriating about fifty neighbors. Why don't you try voodoo instead, Dominique?"

"I've already tried," answered the Frenchwoman, "and it hasn't worked very well. Her car was totaled, but she got out unharmed."

"Keep trying," said the aldermen.

"I can't; something's protecting her," claimed Dominique, opening her billfold and looking at them sternly.

I touched my long hair—dried out and bleached from too much sun—and I gave thanks to Yemanyá. The part about the accident was true. I was driving alone one afternoon at about sixty miles an hour when the breaks had suddenly stopped working. The car crashed and was totaled. I was terribly frightened, but nothing, absolutely nothing, had happened to me.

I told Mariana what I had heard in the Municipality. "Are you willing to give up the part of your patio that is on public land?" she asked me. I said that I would if all of my neighbors surrendered what they had on public land: gardens, hotels, houses, restaurants, and *pulperías*—yes, of course.

The Constitutional Tribunal order only cheered me up a little: it was a vote of confidence in the Minister of Natural Wealth, and it left everything in his hands.

Overcoming strong internal resistance and the memory of something like treason, I called Ana Luisa. I asked her what the Ministry was going to do with the vote of confidence. "We're not going to do anything;" she responded, "private property does not allow restrictions." She was cold and hostile.

I decided to talk with Margarita, the Head of the Legal Department of Parks, the nice, plump woman. At least she was human and affectionate.

Going into the offices that are called "Park System" is a risky operation. I realized that when I called Margarita, and one of the lawyers threw a bucket of cold water on me through the telephone line: "Don't even come here, Daniela; we don't want you here. We had to help the Minister's other lawyers to answer your calumnious, injurious, and obscene appeal. The Minister will fire anyone who talks to you."

That's why I'm in a cold sweat, and I smell like a frightened animal; how can I request information without getting anyone who helps me fired?

Ana Luisa had advised me a long time ago, when I still worked in the Ministry and the Minister was furious because of my letters denouncing him to the Attorney General, that I should buy one of those masks with a huge nose, moustache, and glasses.

Ana Luisa had begged me on the days she wasn't in to please take advantage of my slender form and disguise myself like a man with the false nose, moustache, and eyeglasses if I had to go to my office in the Ministry for any important reason. That way the Minister would not recognize me. And I would thereby avoid getting her in any trouble.

That's why today I arrive at the Park System Office disguised as a big-nosed, moustached, and bespectacled man. But I'm still afraid that someone will discover my disguise.

I introduce myself to the receptionist as Woody Boscoso, and I ask for an appointment with the Head of the Legal Department.

The secretary of the Legal Department comes over and gives me an appointment.

"What did you say your name was, señor?"

"Woody Boscoso, ecotourism expert."

Today, Woody Boscoso, ecotourism expert, has an appointment in the Parks System. Doña Margarita's secretary tells me, "The Head Lawyer is busy, but she will be with you in half an hour."

"Can I wait in that lounge?"

"Yes, of course. Please step in and have a seat."

Suddenly, the man with the ten bypasses appears; my heart starts pounding with fear. Dressed in his leather jacket, he walks in as if he were right at home, followed by the congressman accused of having drafted laws in his own self-interest. They go into an office and close the door.

I listen sharply, but only a murmur is audible.

About half an hour later, the Minister, the artificial man, the congressman, and a Park System lawyer emerge. The secretary informs me, "Please go in, Señor Boscoso; Doña Margarita is ready to see you."

I introduce myself, I greet her, I take out a notebook, and I ask for details about the internationally known parks. She recounts emotionally that the Parks are like her children: she watched them being born; she even helped to deliver them—she is the Parks' midwife. She remarks how sad it is that many of them are dying; they're going to die because unfortunately they're on private property and . . . . I interrupt her because I don't want to hear about the Arenal decision again. I take the opportunity to ask her what she thinks of Daniela Zermat's appeal and whether the Parks System isn't gladdened by a legal action on behalf of nature.

"She and Mariana can't win that appeal because they'll starve three thousand families to death."

I hope that my sudden pallor hasn't surprised her. Starve three thousand families to death? Which ones? My hands are shaking.

"Why do you say that, counsel?"

From sheer fright, I almost forget to deepen my voice.

"What Daniela Zermat is doing is a crime. *She means to stop the community's sustainable development, to deprive them of their right to progress.* What she's doing is a crime."

"But if I haven't misunderstood the appeal . . ."

"Oh, you've read it, Señor Boscoso?"

"I always examine legal actions that are related to nature."

Margarita says that Mariana's legal foundation is very good but full of errors, adding that, for instance, Mariana cites international accords as if the agreements signed by the country could be applied just like that."

"But, Doña Margarita, do you mean, then, that signing them is not really like signing them?"

"Exactly, Señor Boscoso. To sign agreements and not to create laws and norms to give them content is like not having signed them."

I pulled the Constitution out of my pocket and read Article Seven in a loud voice: international accords "will have superior authority to the laws from the time of their promulgation or from the time they so designate."

At that moment the door opened, and a head appeared asking, "Who's shouting?" It was the well-known Medea, the General Legal Head of the Ministry. She entered, introduced herself, and announced to Margarita that the Minister was expecting her for another meeting, but that the conversation was very interesting, for she had heard my shouting from outside, and that she would continue the interview. Margarita left, and Medea explained to me that international accords were only "letters of intention" and could not be applied.

"How curious, Doña Medea. An emeritus judge of the International Court of Human Rights has said that "what explains and justifies international safeguards is precisely the insufficiency of domestic resources.""

"Well, that judge doesn't know a darn thing, Señor Boscoso. Who is it?"

"The Emeritus Thomas Buergenthal, Doña Medea."

"We don't know him here. And if you see Daniela, tell her to watch out. Three thousand families."

"That's strange, because in the accessible part of the Gandoca Refuge, there aren't even two thousand persons. Besides, what Daniela and Mariana want is *not* to detain progress. Quite the contrary. They want to change the current mode of development of the Gandoca Refuge because it isn't sustainable. It can't be sustained. Look, I totally agree with them. The actual development is so difficult to sustain that when I went to see Punta Uva, a man and his jeep had sunk into one of the immense ditches that a Frenchwoman had made to drain her sewage into the sea. When I finished my tour of the area a week later, the jeep was still stuck. They were searching for a bigger tractor to pull it out of the bottom of the hole. When Daniela opposed the construction of that ditch, they wanted to throw her in jail. If the development makes the tourists sink, then it isn't sustainable."

"I haven't seen the ditches, but I completely disagree with you about the inconvenience they constitute. For a North American tourist bored with the uniformity of highways in his country, to fall into a hole in the Gandoca Refuge could be the adventure of his life, Señor Boscoso."

"To regard sinking up to one's neck in sewage as a touristic adventure is questionable, Doña Medea, especially because there's already a cholera epidemic in our country."

Medea sighed and, raising her eyes heavenward, said that it was necessary to demystify sewage. She noted that fecal waste was useful for fertilization and that if foreign capital was regulated, it simply wouldn't come, and then the country would not become developed. Her tone rose as she added, "Daniela's problem is that she lacks tolerance. She's the only person who is making trouble on account of the sewage and the deforestation, the only one. That proves that the development of the Gandoca Refuge is sustainable; what's going on is that Daniela doesn't know anything about economics; she gets furious with us because we're going to save the country a vast outflow of currency: we're going to put the equivalent of Miami in the Gandoca Wildlife Refuge."

"Miami? Then Daniela's right."

"No, she's not right to attack us, precisely because it is going to be an ecological Miami. It's a marvelous project that we're presenting to the International Monetary Fund and the Inter-American Development Bank, a project for which the President could win the Nobel Prize for Economy and for Ecology. Can you imagine the continual savings of currency that is now spent abroad, as well as the immense profits that an ecological commercial center will bring to one of the poorest parts of our country!"

"I would love to know more about that project, Doña Medea."

"When it's ready, I'll send it to you. Look, I'm saying that Daniela doesn't know her fellow citizens: as soon as the Costa Ricans earn a few bucks, they seek to invest them in a condo in Florida with all of the amenities. They're not going to bother going into a jungle where there's no television, cabarets, dance clubs, or stores—an unhealthy, horrible jungle where they could be infected by *leichmaniasis*,[3] measles, cholera, or malaria. Señor Boscoso, let's speak frankly: conservationists look rather suspiciously like leftists, don't they? They're opposed to progress. Capitalism is the only form of possible progress now. Socialism has died. So, it's a simple logical deduction: they're opposed to capitalism; *ergo* they're communists, don't you see? We want the best for our country, and that's why we defend technology, foreign capital, the benefits of touristic development such as in Spain or in Mexico, countries that are getting excellent results. Señor Boscoso, do you know the Minister of Mass Tourism?"

"Yes, I . . ."

---

[3] A tropical disease also known as "leper of the jungle." [Tr.]

"He's a brilliant man. He just invented the universal definition of ecotourism: "Where the hotels are no higher than the tallest palm tree." What do you think, Señor Boscoso? Isn't it just wonderful? I'm pulling strings to try to get it included in the second edition of the Ecological Dictionary. Our country could be saved by that definition."

"Saved from what?"

"From skyscrapers. Señor Boscoso, as our Minister of Mass Tourism so well puts it, it's a crime to oppose a dazzling hotel project of the kind that has transparent pools, thousands of air-conditioned rooms, hot water, broad paved avenues instead of dusty backroads, and elegant restaurants with dishes of international cuisine, on the alleged basis that it destroys a few trees, indigenous cemeteries, or our cultural and historical heritage. Can, by chance, our people eat from those trees or from those funeral urns or statues? How can you stop something so extraordinary as a great investment of millions of dollars for the sole and senseless reason that it is probably illegal?"

"Daniela, stop disguising yourself as Woody Boscoso," Mariana tells me. "They could discover you at any moment. Here's a report about an important meeting that was held in the Ministry to deal with the housing developments in the Gandoca Refuge. Take it and read it right now."

The Minister and some of his advisors met with the Italians of the "Ecodollars Company, Inc."

"Esteemed investors," said the Minister, "we have to look at an intelligent alternative in case the Environmental Impact Study and the Forestry or Wildlife Law requires us to reduce the housing development a bit."

"But you had told us that anything would be permitted because it is private property," asserted a lawyer from the "Ecodollars" Company, Inc.

"Wellll, yes, I still hold to that belief, but it wouldn't hurt to reinforce the concept of the housing development positively—as we say here, to 'tie' it to higher levels so that your project will be more attractive than any environmentalist alternative such as putting up bungalows without cutting many trees, and stupidities of that sort. Let's see, Señor Gonzalez, please explain the idea."

The Minister's advisor got up, cleared his throat, and said, "My proposal is to play with economic weapons and with the same weapons that the greens use. To begin with, the housing development and shopping centers will be ecologically 'green.' Consider this: one of our government's objectives is to secure stable, long-range income. Now our country loses millions of dollars every year because of the Costa Ricans who travel to Miami for shopping, especially during the Christmas season. We're going to provide the government with hard currency and the effective savings of at least half of those dollars by building a Miami in the Gandoca Refuge. A Jungle Miami. Besides ice-skating rinks, there will be all of the same stores as in Miami and Florida but with an ecological slant: a Jungle Burdine's, a Jungle J. C. Penney, a . . ."

"But," ventured another person, "there won't be any jungle . . ."

"Oh yes, that's true. I hadn't thought about that minor detail. So let's say a Green Burdine's, a Green J. C. Penney . . . an ecological McDonald's, an ecological dance club constructed with 100% soundproof materials so that the noise won't bother the birds . . ."

"But," ventured the same person again, "if there's no jungle, there won't be any birds either. . . ."

"There won't be any jungle, but there will be trees. Don't you see, we're planning to have green reforested areas with native species such as the Honduran Pine, the eucalyptus . . ."

"Those aren't native species."

"Look, Señor, your objections seem suspicious. You aren't a communist, are you? We'll look for the native species and plant those."

"Excuse me, I'm not a communist but a biologist, and I know that if the habitat changes, the native species won't be able to develop, because they need . . ."

. "We'll plant the species that we can!" shouted the exasperated advisor. "As I was saying, the President will present the project to the International Monetary Fund and the Inter-American Development Bank with an intelligent plan such as a Nature-for-Debt Swap—I mean, excuse me, a Debt-for-Nature Swap. It will surely be approved, not only because of the cash savings brought about by Costa Ricans doing their shopping in the Gandoca Refuge, but also because it will be Green, which is the latest fashion, and we'll capture thousands of tourists from other places who will come to spend a Green Christmas. The poor inhabitants of New England who freeze during their White Christmases will come to enjoy a Green Christmas, and they'll be able to taste all of the dishes that they're used to eating up there: oysters, turkeys, . . ."

"There are almost no oysters left in the Gandoca Refuge now. . . . The genetic bank of mangrove oyster is at the point of extinction."

"We'll import them."

"In the long range, that is not healthy for the economy."

"Then we'll establish oyster farms in the Refuge, and that way we'll provide work for the area's fishermen."

One of the Minister's advisors happily clapped his hands together, saying, "How delicious to eat big American oysters."

"In debt-for-nature swaps, do we give up nature and remain stuck with the debt, or is it the opposite: do we give up the debt and retain nature?" asked one of the Minister's advisors.

No one wanted to answer him.

The Italian investor was visibly upset. The Minister calmed him, saying in a low voice, "The commercial centers will be yours, and you'll rent the sites to Burdine's, etc."

The Italian's face brightened. Everyone left the meeting content with the project except the biologist, who kept wondering what would remain of the habitat.

"The biologist is my friend," said Mariana. "The 'Ecodollars' Company is certain that no one can stop its project."

"Not even if we win the appeal?"

"It looks as though that Green Miami will be established even if we win the appeal."

"But how is that possible?"

"I don't know, I don't know. Holy Mother, Daniela, how helpless we are."

I'm exhausted. And when I get home, I still have to take off my make-up, pull genial Juan Boscoso's nose off my own, remove the glued-on eyebrows and thick moustache. . . .

Disguising myself as Woody Boscoso brings in a sense of humor, which is to say, perspective, so that wretchedness and discouragement don't devour me, or so that they at least don't devour me as quickly. But disguising myself as Woody Boscoso also wears me out.

When I open the door, my youngest son bursts out in side-splitting laughter: "Here comes Mommy disguised as a man."

He thinks that it is a game that I am doing just for him; he's only three years old. I pick him up, kiss him, and tell him that I'm his uncle Woody Boscoso. He pulls my moustache, and we have fun for a while with the character. Sometimes I'm so tired that I sit down to eat with the children without taking off my disguise. Anita, the maid, is worried, and she keeps casting glances at me while serving dinner.

When I get home today, it's not my youngest son who comes out to greet me but you, my friend. I had not told you about my alter ego Woody Boscoso, and you are quite shocked.

"No, I'm not crazy; let me explain."

Behind you, I hear the children's howls of laughter.

You demand that I take off the disguise before eating. You've come to eat with us, and you have brought special dishes—chop suey and chow mein—from the Chinese restaurant that my children love. You persuade me that it's a special occasion, and that as a result you have the right to demand to eat with Daniela, not Woody Boscoso. I tell you that that's a shame, because Woody could tell you what happened today. . . .

"Let's talk about something else, woman. Come here."

You take me to the laundry room. You look for the creams, and you diligently press me to remove my make-up.

"You're going to ruin your skin. Oh, Daniela, Daniela, you're so beautiful and so crazy."

"Don't call me 'crazy,' because that's like what they call me in the Ministry—'the madwoman of Gandoca.'"

"Your madness is good; it's your most charming feature."

"But it's not madness. Don't repeat that."

"Excuse me; I didn't mean it in a pejorative sense, quite the contrary."

During the meal, I remember that the "Ecodollars" company has already bought the electric transformers for the housing development and has given the Ministry and the Municipality the truck that will pick up the garbage and throw it into the rivers, and so, even though the chow mein is delicious, I can't swallow a bite. You ask me to explain what the conservationist groups are doing to help me.

"Apart from the logistical help that the Association for Water and the Foundation for the Environment has given me . . ."

"No, I mean the NGOs that work in the area."

"Nothing, they haven't done anything. They're not going to do anything."

"Explain that to me. Have you gone to see them?"

"Yes, yes, I went to see them. One was the Alchemists Association, which was established in the Gandoca Refuge at the time of its creation. They told me, 'We already have too many problems to take on a fight with the Minister. Besides, we've already given too much money for that Refuge. For example, we pay the Administrator.'

"'There is no Administrator.'

"'We still pay him. Look, we've tried to take care of this Refuge, but an NGO can do nothing if the state uses its power to block the administrative measures that the NGO proposes. That's what has happened to us. You yourself admit that you used to see controls. Well, the few controls that we were once permitted have been stripped from us.'

"'But you should be fighting back and demanding planning and regulation.'

"'But the lawyer from our organization says that not even a single law can be applied to the Refuge.'

"'That's not true.'

"'It must be true. She knows an awful lot.'

"'We initiated the appeal because five articles of the Political Constitution are directly applicable to the Refuge, as well as seven international agreements, which have greater weight than the law. There are also two laws: the Forestry

Law and the Wildlife Law, not to mention the Refuge Creation and Regulation Act.'

"'You don't say!'

"'Oh, and the American Convention on Human Rights is also applicable.'

"'What's that?'"

"After my failure with the Alchemists Association, I went to the well-known Nature Conservation Union. I was told there that they preferred not to enter into conflict with the Ministry. They added a moment later that the Minister should be excused because it wasn't his fault, and because he had simply received a messianic command."

"'He received a messianic command to destroy the Refuge?'" I asked them.

"The NCU officials nodded their sage heads in agreement."

After hearing those two accounts and the sadness in my voice, my children don't want to eat anymore. They suddenly discover a strange taste in the chow mein. You, my friend, get angry: "Stop telling them tragedies; you're going to make them sick."

But this is my "fleeing forward," my *fuite en avant*, and I can't stop. I add, "Oh, you should hear what happened to me on the way to . . ."

"Tell me some other day, Daniela. Please, let's talk about nice things."

But the children, their eyes as wide as dishes, want me to go on.

"Well, Woody Boscoso was sad as he was coming back today, thinking of the things I told you about, the transformers, the garbage trucks, and all that. There is a beautiful place on the way here that is my solace. It's an old and beautiful house that has been declared National Historical Heritage: it's the House of Fountains. Well, this afternoon I was in urgent need of those labyrinths of stone and moss and water. When I got there, I found a steamroller demolishing the walls. The fountains no longer existed; there were only mounds of debris with the pipes pulled up. I went immediately to the Ministry of Culture to ask on what grounds the Historical Heritage was being demolished. They answered, 'It's because the owner needs it to make a parking lot. The government has no funds for expropriation. . . .'

"'But it's Historical Heritage; why don't you ask the owner to restore it instead of demolishing it and to make something more attractive and lucrative than a parking lot?'

"'Because it's private property. Private property cannot be limited, even if it's Historical Heritage.' That is what the employee from the Ministry of Culture said."

I am with my children in the music room. The eldest, Andreas, is playing Debussy's "The Sunken Cathedral" on the piano. He knows that it is one of the pieces that I most enjoy. His virtuoso fingers fill the air with a modernist current that amuses me.

The second child studies some scores and waits for Andreas to finish before beginning his alto saxophone practice. And the little one leans his round cheeks against my shoulder and asks me for a story. It relieves me to think that in a world of market values, I was at least able to give them an inner life.

"Doña Daniela," the maid interrupts us, "a young man is looking for you."

"I'm busy. Ask him what he wants."

"He insisted that it was urgent. Very urgent."

"Okay, I'm on my way."

"Doña Daniela, how are you? Excuse me for interrupting you and your family on a Sunday. My name is Máinor Rojas, and I have just been given the position of Agent in Charge of Refuges in the Ministry. I don't know if you knew that they have just moved the Refuges to the Wildlife Office."

"It's nice to meet you, Máinor. Hey, the Refuges have danced through seven offices in less than a year, so I have lost track of them, and I don't remember whether they were in Forestry or in Wildlife in the last chapter."

"Look, I've come to you because I desperately need your help."

"My help? I am a *persona non grata* in the Ministry. Besides, I'm up to here with it, utterly saturated. I don't want to hear anything about Gandoca for a long time. Call me in a couple of weeks. Right now I'm listening to 'The Sunken Cathedral.'"

"No, please don't go! I need your help. It's very urgent. You know, a lot of lumber has been taken from the last remaining forests of the Gandoca Refuge."

"Illegally, Máinor. I've seen the trucks pass by full of logs."

"Some of it has also been legal. The Limón Forestry Office authorizes the cutting and registry without consulting the central Forestry Office, Daniela."

"Even if they consult the Forestry Office in San José, they get permission."

"But at least they keep a record. In any event, I presented myself at the Limón Forestry Office, browbeat them, and carried off the timber files for the Gandoca Refuge and surrounding areas. Then I ordered them to halt everything while I study the situation."

"You're a brave man."

Yes, Máinor seemed a brave man, and I stayed to talk to him while Andreas continued playing "The Sunken Cathedral" on the piano. Máinor said that he had arrived at the Limón Forestry Office in the sultry humidity of mid-morning and requested all the lumber files. The inspectors didn't want to give them to him. He had to snatch them from the inspectors. With the files in hand, he discovered that sixty-four people were already removing or intended to remove lumber from the Gandoca Refuge and surrounding areas.

"Oh, shit, sixty-four is too many. You had better call the Vice-Minister and leave me to 'The Sunken Cathedral.'"

"No, no, look, the Vice-Minister either can't or won't do anything. I estimate that if these misnamed 'forestry uses' are permitted, 1500 acres of primary forest will be lost. You know that it's our last remaining tract. The new Administrator of the Gandoca Refuge and I . . ."

"They've finally named an Administrator? How lucky."

Máinor says that he and the new Administrator went to see the trees that were being cut. From the moment they entered the first farm, they noticed a melodious gurgle. According to Máinor, that melodious gurgle never left them for a moment because the lumber permits solicited were all for sites near springs, rivers, or lakes.

I recalled that the teacher from the fishermen's town had said that they were going to cut the forests that protected the water supply.

"Daniela, I need an intelligent lawyer to help me deny all or part of these permits."

"Máinor, the person you need is Mariana."

Máinor and Mariana met. She told him that forests near springs, river-beds, or slopes were protected areas *per se*, even if they hadn't been declared as such. She reminded him, "Máinor, according to the law of this country, there are four types of protected land: the first two, the National Parks and the Biological Reserves, are untouchable state property; the third, the Wildlife Refuges, are mixed; and the last, the Protected Areas, are ones in which the owner doesn't lose title to the property, and the state imposes limitations that it deems necessary, at least according to a recent decision by the First Tribunal. The permit requests that you have shown me all lie in Protected Areas *per se*."

"Exactly."

"Okay, then, we have to base our work on the First Tribunal's decision, imposing limitations on private property to protect the water."

"I would prefer to deny the permits altogether. The trees are in such fragile places that they won't withstand even careful handling."

Máinor desperately called us again. He says that he denied the lumbering permits and that Medea, the General Legal Head of the whole Ministry, became furious. She called him into her office and told him in a strident voice that he should get it through his head once and for always that to say no in this country was unconstitutional. Máinor, hanging by a thread, said that Medea was forcing him to approve the permits.

"No, Máinor," said Mariana. "I studied the documentation carefully. The farms where they want to cut have new property titles from the Agrarian Institute. Take a close look, and you'll see that the titles exclude forest utilization for five years. You can deny the permits without any problem."

"Oh, that's great."

But like a fairy tale full of curses embodied in repetitive formulas, Máinor desperately called us again, because he had denied the permits on the basis of the clause in the title deed, and then the Forestry Office intervened, saying that the clause was unconstitutional, that common practice was the law, and that they had always granted the permits before the five years were up—what's more, they had done so in two days.

"I don't doubt it; that's why this country is in such bad shape," I commented.

"Look, Máinor, don't despair," Mariana told him. "Grant the permits with the limitations permitted by law in fragile areas. For example, the wood must be carried out by oxen, and not by machines, etc. But then be sure to send an inspector to see if the woodcutters are actually observing the limitations. And if they're not respecting them, revoke the permits."

"Of course, of course, what an excellent idea."

But once again the maleficent, repetitive, bewitched formula returned: Máinor's call. We got together.

"And now what?" Mariana asked him.

"They moved the Refuges to the Forestry Office again, and . . ."

"Eight!" Mariana and I shouted in unison.

"Eight what?" asked Máinor, startled.

"Eight different offices in one year; the refuges have danced through eight offices, and they keep dancing. If this were a novel and not actual truth, they would say that the author was abusing *deus ex machina*," I explained.

But Máinor said that he wished that that were all, for the Minister had also taken the Gandoca lumber files from his hands and returned them to the Forestry Office in Limón. Mariana advised him not to worry but to help the Limón technicians establish restrictions and to supervise them. Máinor explained that Medea was roundly opposed to restrictions. Mariana told him, "Take advantage of the fact that Medea doesn't work in Limón, and go and try to persuade the technicians there. Take them to see the trees; take them to hear the melodious gurgle."

"They won't let me take them, and they don't like to go to the Gandoca Refuge."

"No, they don't like to. They say that they get lost," I reminded them.

"Yes, it has also been my experience that they get lost and never arrive," corroborated Máinor.

Mariana then suggested that he send them a compass.

Once again we witness the power of the curse, the enchanted words that transformed princes into toads and forests into treeless wastes, the monotonous repetition of the song. A desperate Máinor reports that the technicians of Limón agreed to go to the Gandoca Refuge but that their compass didn't work. After they passed Puerto Viejo, north was deviated by the magnetic sand, the black sand that has little magnets in it. Máinor recounts that he then sent them a stronger, steadier compass. That didn't work for them either. There is no way for them to arrive or to impose restrictions, which means that they are even less able to supervise them. There will be no way.

I had had enough of the situation in the Gandoca Refuge, but I didn't want to stand there with my arms crossed and do nothing. They were the forests that I most loved; besides, there was the whole matter of their biodiversity.

I called a newspaper reporter and explained the problem to him. I showed him the loggers' permit requests, which I had diligently photocopied—they were, after all, public documents—, and I showed him the judgment of biologists and engineers certifying the fragility of the areas. The reporter went to investigate. In addition, I wrote a strong letter of protest to the Minister, and sent a copy to everyone in the country, including the Defender of Human Rights, the *Contralor*,[4] the congresspersons, etc., to see if these VIPs would make him protect the springs.

A few days later a long article in the paper appeared, documenting the disaster by the Offices of Refuges and of Forestry and denouncing the imminent loss of 1500 acres of forest in the South of Limón. The reporter had done a good job, and the VIPs had become interested and pressured the Minister to protect the springs. For the first time in a year and a half, I slept peacefully.

---

[4] An official charged with examining government contracts with private enterprise. [Tr.]

But the next day, another long article appeared with a picture of Máinor denying everything, with a picture of the Forestry Director—not the Superior Director but the other one—, affirming that the reporter's information was an abject lie, that the whole thing was a set-up, that there was no cutting, that there was no disaster, that there was no spring, and that everything was being taken care of, arranged, put in order. It assured the VIPs that everything was under control, that the forests were intact, and that Refuges and Forestry were swimming along marvelously.

"Máinor, why did you deny everything, why, why, why?"

"The Minister was as mad as the devil and ordered me to, as did the Forestry Director. They both threatened to fire me."

"But why did they lie?"

"Because the Minister says that the only thing you're after is to discredit selfless public officials."

"And now what's going to happen to the trees?"

"I don't know, Daniela. I can't risk losing my job."

In a year and a half and by virtue of repeated blows, I had discovered what was going on in this country. The governments paid lip service to assure the entire world that twenty-eight percent of the territory was under some type of protection. And when someone actually went to the Ministry of Natural Wealth to ask it to exercise this protection, the Ministry would answer that it was impossible and that the only thing that could be protected was what was called "heritage of the Costa Ricans": the Parks that had been actually expropriated and paid for. So it wasn't twenty-eight percent but rather less than ten percent of the territory that was protected. And, moreover, that ten percent was at the point of dying. Sonorous and evocative names of green turtles—Tortuguero—, trees that bleed in cycles like women—Cahuita—, transparent arms of the sea—Manuel

Antonio—, or colonial treasures—La Isla del Coco—were threatened by thousands of tons of garbage and of pesticides, merciless clearcutting, illegal concessions to foreign companies, and droves of devastating mega-tourist developments.

I remembered that according to scientists, Costa Rican soil is being lost at a rate of four million tons a year. And certain statistics show that we have the highest deforestation rate on earth.

We sit on the seashore. It's a sunny afternoon in Playa Chiquita. I am with Robinson, my three children, and Gloria, a descendent of ancient Cabécar or Bribri chiefs. Robinson asks me when the Constitutional Tribunal will decide whether or not to support my appeal. I answer that the Constitutional Tribunal's decision could take years. Robinson comments that it will be too late by then— too late for the Gandoca Refuge.

"That's because of the leaf-cutting ants," the Indian daughter suggests. "My Bribri and Cabécar relatives once said the following in a proclamation called, 'Caring for the Gifts of God': 'There is a big difference between the indian and the white man. Watch the leaf-cutting ants—how all of them work together, clean, and care for their territory. Wherever the leaf-cutters live, everything is clean, because they cut all of the leaves and make their big nests. The white man is like that; he works very hard, but he destroys nature. He keeps cleaning, cleaning, cleaning everything out to make his cities, but where he lives, nothing exists. The white cuts down everything that is green and wild, and where he lives, no trees or rivers remain.'"[5]

---

[5] Taken from the book Cuidando los regalos de Dios: testimonios de la Reserva Indígena Cocles/Kekoldi (Eng. Caring for the Gifts of God: Testimonies from the Cocles/Kekoldi Indigenous Reserve), p. 16. Written by Paula Palmer, Juanita Sánchez, and Gloria Mayorga and published by La Vicerrectoría de Acción Social, Universidad de Costa Rica, San José, Costa Rica, 1988. [Au.]

Gloria says that the *awapa* have been dreaming a bad dream. They have seen Talamanca destroyed.

But we shouldn't despair, says my oldest child.

Andreas is filled with hope just by watching the tense line of a palm tree bent by the wind. He believes in life. He's only twelve years old.

He hasn't passed through love and death, like I have. He hasn't passed through slavery and race-misery, like Robinson. He hasn't been dispossessed, like Gloria.

Robinson's voice acquires a solemn tone. He tells me, "Daniela, a few months ago when the man with the ten bypasses or his friends threatened to burn your house and you came to my office to tell me, you said: *"Me queda la palabra*—I still have words, the power of speech, the chance to be heard." And Beto, your friend from Cahuita, observed that that's a lot, because we blacks haven't even had that. And Beto then added, 'History is words.' You said, 'Yes, but written words.' And the thing is, Daniela, that we blacks haven't ever been given the floor, so to speak; no one has cared to listen even to our spoken words, the ones that the wind carries off."

Robinson gets up, points toward the sea, and commands me, "Right now you're going to begin to write it. Don't let it vanish in the air, like the melancholy shout of the emerald toucanet.

I mind him. I get up, go home, grab pen and paper, and begin. A knot forms in my throat. I start at the beginning. I write, "You hated boleros, Carlos Manuel . . ."

Afterword

In 1995, three years after the publication of the novel, the Constitutional Tribunal ruled in favor of Anacristina Rossi's appeal to save the rich marine area of the refuge. It also ruled in favor of Melania Agüero, another courageous woman who had presented an appeal against uncontrolled development and irrational logging in the wildlife refuge. These victories meant not only improved prospects for the future of the wildlife refuge, but also an important change in legislation. After the Arenal decision, private property had been regarded by government officials as not subject to any regulations, even if located within protected areas such as wildlife refuges. But through these latest rulings, the Constitutional Tribunal made it clear that the protection of the environment is for the common good of all citizens, who are endowed with the right to enjoy a healthy environment (their "derecho al ambiente") and that economic considerations, such as the need for development, are secondary to those pertaining to the common good. It also stated that individual citizens, as well as the government, are responsible for the conservation of the "ecological patrimony" of Costa Rica for generations to come.

Unfortunately, these achievements were never translated into real practice. According to Costa Rican law, the person who wins the appeal is expected to pressure the government to follow suit. But at this time Anacristina Rossi received death threats and was forced to leave the country temporarily. Big investors and a political system riddled by bureaucracy, corruption, and apathy were too great a challenge for one person alone to overcome.

In December1996, the MINAE (Ministry for Energy and the Environment) published a Management Plan for the GMWR, created with local communities and organizations. Its purpose is to "optimally manage the natural resources and the environment under the most strict sustainable development principles in harmony with nature." To accomplish this, it divides the refuge into 15 major zones, each one with recommended and conditional uses. The maps show that most of the lands (zones 2 to 15) are for research and conservation. However, these lands also allow certain conditional uses such as agriculture, forestry exploitation, and single-family houses. This detailed management plan shows an effort on the part of the Costa Rican government to balance development and conservation. Unfortunately, it does not address the major problem that Rossi pondered in her novel, which is the conflict between private land ownership and conservation. To this day, more than ninety percent of the lands of the refuge are owned by individuals, most of them foreigners. And its protection is left largely to their good will in voluntarily following the general zoning rules.

Since 2000, the GMWR has faced yet another threat: the Costa Rican government granted concessions to two North American corporations, Harken Energy and Mallon Oil, to explore for oil on the entire Costa Rican Caribbean sea bottom. These concessions occurred without consultation of the local population and thereby outraged many people in Limón as well as elsewhere in the country. According to marine scientists, as well as local fishermen, preliminary high-energy seismic explorations done throughout 2000 affected marine mammals, lobster and other ocean species. Moreover, if oil is indeed found, the locals in the Southern Caribbean area (where the GMWR is located) are sure to suffer water, soil, and air contamination. They worry about the future of their ecotourist industry.

Fortunately, people's outrage was quickly channeled into a surprisingly strong anti-oil movement, which has achieved some stunning results in the past five years. Spearheaded by ADELA (Acción de lucha antipetrolera/ Anti-oil Exploration Action), a coalition of 30 citizen organizations that publishes informative leaflets and brochures and has a two-tiered action plan working at the local and international levels, the anti-oil movement won a major victory in May

2002 when President Abel Pacheco, responding to the large-scale mobilization, announced a moratorium on all oil exploration in the country. A battle between Harken and the Costa Rican government ensued and continues today. Harken has tried several times to intimidate Costa Rican law makers, first by suing the country for 57 billion dollars in damages, and then by trying to reach an out-of-court settlement. But these efforts have been met by the anti-oil movement's unrelenting commitment to protect the Caribbean natural environment. They continue challenging rulings that clearly do not serve local and national interests.

Despite the apparent strength of the environmental movement, one wonders about Costa Rica's long-term prospects. Since 2005, when Costa Rica joined CAFTA, the Central American Free Trade Agreement, Costa Ricans have become both acutely aware and fearful of the power of international corporations to trump local environmental laws. As has been the case with NAFTA, CAFTA empowers international corporations to sue for lost, projected or actual, profits. And with presidential elections in 2006, many fear that the oil business will finally gain access to the area. There certainly is a circularity of events reminiscent of the circularity of the story line of *La loca de Gandoca*. The same way the text starts and ends in a call for action, the reality of the Caribbean coast seems to call for a never-ending battle to keep its natural and cultural wealth intact.

Today, when visiting the GMWR, it is obvious that the balance promised by the zoning plan has not been achieved. Deforestation and population encroachment are happening everywhere in the refuge. Even Punta Mona (Monkey Point), considered the jewel of the refuge for its wetlands and primary forests, is deteriorating. Although most of its glorious trees are still standing, one can see the signs of human interference at many points: unsightly barbwire fences indicating property boundaries, underbrush clearings, and in one remote area, a tract of land completely clearcut from hill to sea by an owner who wanted the sea breezes to reach his house on the top of a hill. Some people believe that this forest remains only because there is no access road to it. Others believe that some landowners realize that ecotourists are paying good money to see this forest and its amazing biodiversity and that therefore it is in their best interest to leave the woods alone.   Whatever the reason, in the absence of stricter conservation measures, the future of the refuge remains precarious at best and subject to economic pressures. Many conservationists believe that expropriation is the only way Punta Mona can be kept pristine. The zoning plan, although restrictive of many activities in this area, is not adequate because it gives too much weight to property owners' rights to profit from their investments and possessions. As Anacristina Rossi put it in an interview in 1998, "If this place is not given absolute protection, it is going to become just a nice place to visit, as many in the Caribbean, but not a conservation area."

Sofía Kearns